Some of the people you will meet…

Claire

I stop. How does he know my name? I slowly turn around and see him – really see him – for the first time. His extended hand quivers, his bloodshot eyes crusted with sleep-stuff, his clothes threadbare. I fumble with my purse and get out my last twenty dollars. I hand it to the old man. "Here, get yourself something to eat."

Devon

The twenty is burning a hole in my jeans and we sit down on the low brick wall at the mall entrance to decide what to do with it. We kick our legs in uneven rhythm while we debate the best use of the money.

Susie

He smiles. Our hands connect for a minute and I feel his warmth seep into my finger tips, then the contact is lost and he is waiting for his change. I pass over three bucks and a handful of coins and then with a wave and a final thanks he goes out the door, gets into his cab and drives off.

David

I know I could admit it and he would believe me, would give me the twenty back and leave Jefferson and me alone for the rest of the school year. I could tell him that, but it would take more from me than twenty bucks to believe Jay-23 is my real brother.

… and many more!

Also by Elmore Hammes

The Holmes & Watson Mysterious Objects and Events Consortium: The Case of the Witch's Talisman

I really enjoyed the book and I think it would appeal to many middle-school readers. It is suggested for 10-14 but I think down to age 8 would also greatly enjoy it. Fun book for young readers.
-- Beth Cummings, ArmchairInterviews.com

In this absolutely delightful read we meet two young friends who will immediately capture your heart... I really liked this book; it has all the elements of a great mystery read and more. The characters are well developed, the story engaging, the locals very descriptive, and the ending superb... Great mix! Great read! Recommended.
-- Shirley Johnson, Senior Review,
Midwest Book Review

Interesting and fun. It will have the readers trying puzzle out what the talisman is and how Kevin and Ginny can win against the witch. Elmore Hammes has done well with this book.
-- Susie Morris, Amazon Review

Hammes writes well, with fully-fleshed out characters, realistic dialogue, and finely honed perception of the inner lives of his young characters. Any younger reader is sure to find this book an exciting, satisfying read. Highly recommended.
-- Karen Hudson, Amazon Review

The Twenty Dollar Bill

by

Elmore Hammes

The Twenty Dollar Bill

Copyright © 2007 by Elmore Hammes

All Rights Reserved.

* * *

Published by

KANAPOLIS FOG PUBLISHING EMPORIUM

Anderson, Indiana

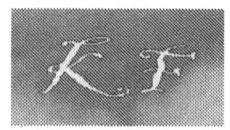

* * *

FIRST PRINTING

ISBN-13: 978-0-6151-4716-1

ISBN-10: 0-615-14716-X

Library of Congress Control Number: 2007906786

*Dedicated to the people
who have touched my life,
in great ways and small,
knowingly and unknowingly,
for the better and for the worse,
as that is what life
is all about.*

C laire

Life just works out. That's what they always say. Not the way we plan, or the way we want it to, but I really think it works out the way it was meant to. How else would people get by in this crazy world? How else would two people who never had a chance of knowing each other, of even meeting, get drawn together, fall in love, live happily ever after?

Maybe it would be best to start at the beginning. Not the real beginning, but mine. Not even my beginning, I guess, but it seems like this is when things started. The reason it was even possible.

It wasn't a dark or stormy night – from the weather you would think it was going to be the best day of your life. Sunny, real comfortable in the mid-seventies, just enough of a breeze to keep the air fresh around you. Perfect. Just like life. Yeah, right. So there I am, minding my own business in this wonderful weather, trying to remember where my bus stop is as I exit the mall, when this smelly, dirt-covered old man walks up to me with his hand out.

Don't get me wrong. I wasn't judging him, I wasn't saying to myself he should go get a job, or even a bath. All I was thinking was I am running late and I have to get home in time to change for my dead-end job at the diner and here's this smelly old guy trying to make me late. Nothing judgmental, as you can see. That's just normal, practical, 'why are you messing with my life when I don't even know you' logic.

So I shake my head and avoid eye contact as I push past him, trying not to breathe in while in his vapor zone. As soon as the old man has passed the extension of my peripheral vision he is out of my thoughts, and I am again wondering if traffic will keep me from making it to Ted's Diner on time.

"Claire."

I stop. How does he know my name? I slowly turn around and see him – really see him – for the first time. His extended hand quivers, his bloodshot eyes crusted with sleep-stuff, his clothes threadbare. I fumble with my purse and get out my last twenty dollars. I hand it to the old man. "Here, get yourself something to eat."

The old man smiles at me as he clutches the twenty. His fetid breath causes me to take a step back. I see the hurt in his eyes at my reaction. I force a smile as I feel my face burn in embarrassment. I step back toward him. His eyes widen, not sure if I am going to strike at him or take the money back. Instead I hug him.

At first he is stiff, but then I feel his whole body relax and he circles his arms around me and hugs me as if he has been waiting to hug someone all his life. We stay like that for I don't know how long – five, ten, fifteen minutes? I think it might have been for hours, but the mall security guard interrupts us.

"Hey, lady, you okay?"

As if waking up from a dream, I blink my eyes and slowly release the old man from my embrace.

"What did I tell you about bugging people, Joe?" The security guard takes a step toward the old man.

"No, no, it's okay. He wasn't bothering me," I assure him. "He wasn't bothering me at all."

The security guard stays where he is, lets the old man walk on. I notice he watches until the bus picks me up.

Those five or ten minutes with the old man, that was the start: I miss my usual transfer. Traffic is slow. The hug ate up all my cushion, and I am late for work. Not a good thing, third time in less than a week. I've been warned. This will cost me my job, and frankly there aren't a whole lot of things I am qualified to do.

J^{oe}

I think that it is going to be a good day. A young lady with a name tag that reads 'Claire' turns around and gives me a twenty, and I think, 'Joe, you are going right down to Ponderosa and eating for three straight hours.' That's what I thought. Them darn kids had other ideas though.

She scares me when she comes in close. I had it happen enough times to know that when someone gets that tight they're coming back after the money, that they just realized it wasn't a one dollar bill they handed you. But then it wasn't about the money at all. Then she wraps her arms around me and once I realize she isn't attacking me I put mine around her. It is heaven, it is like holding and being held by an angel, and I feel thirty years of living on my own roll right off my back, and the warmth – good God, the warmth – soaks through my body like it has never been cold.

After what seems like hours some mall cop comes up and drives the angel away. I feel the warmth in my bones though, even after she has walked off to the bus stop. Even after the mall cop suggests I find somewhere else to bum around.

I head across the crowded parking lot. Ponderosa is a half block away, and my stomach churns as I think about filling it overfull for the first time in months. I am so lost in thoughts of all-you-can-eat buffets that I do not notice the kids coming at me from the side.

"Hey, old man, what'cha got there?"

I turn to see a greasy haired punk carrying a skateboard, with two more just like him at his side. I follow his pointed finger down to my hands to see I am still clutching the gift twenty dollar bill, held out for all the world to see. I curse inside at my foolishness.

"My lunch money," I offer. I smile, hoping to convey strength, courage or confidence to the kids – anything that will let me keep the money.

"Ah, don't'cha know it's past lunch time?"

"Yeah, man, don't'cha know that?" another kid pipes in.

"Ponderosa is still open," I say. I try to resume my walk but the kids step in front of me, blocking the way.

"Please, it's all I have. I'm hungry. Just leave me alone, let me go and have myself a good meal." They hesitate and I try to drive my point home. "I haven't eaten in three days. A lady just gave me this money. She wanted me to get something to eat with it. Please let me do that. Don't throw her mercy away."

The smallest kid shuffles his feet. "Maybe we should..."

The skateboard-carrying kid sneers. "Should what? Let this old man get away with stealing. I don't believe that crap about some lady giving him twenty bucks. Look at him! There's no way anyone would give him money. He stole it."

"No, I swear, she gave it to me. She gave me the money and she hugged me."

The kid laughs. "See, what'd I tell ya? No way in hell anyone would hug him. I can hardly stand being this close to him."

The other kids laugh and nod their heads at his statement. The leader reaches out and grabs the twenty from me. I want to grab it back, I want to shout for help, but I know the only help is what I have already received. The warmth of the angel is still in my bones. I guess I don't really need any food in my stomach.

D^{evon}

So we are bumming around the mall, trying to avoid getting run off by the rent-a-cops when we see the old man. What a screwy geezer, walking like he is asleep, holding that twenty dollar bill in front of him like it is some kind of trophy.

I look at Skeeter and Tom and we just laugh out loud. Easy pickings, it would be a crime not to teach the old guy a lesson. If it wasn't us it would be somebody else parting that bill from him, and they wouldn't be so nice about it.

He tries to give us some sort of sob story, and man, Skeeter starts shuffling around and looking like he is going to believe it. As if some lady would have hugged this guy! God, it is all I can do to avoid puking, he smells so bad, I can't imagine touching the geezer.

But that money, that smells just fine. So I tell Skeeter and Tom how the old man is the real thief, that we are just teaching him a lesson. Once they see how stupid the old man's story is they realize I am right. After I grab the bill from him we take off across the parking lot, leaving the old guy mumbling something about angels and Ponderosa.

We see the rent-a-cop when we get to the other side of the parking lot. Tom flips him the bird and he starts coming our way. We all wave in a three finger salute and then duck around the cars until he gives up chasing us.

The twenty is burning a hole in my jeans and we sit down on the low brick wall at the mall entrance to decide what to do with it. We kick our legs in uneven rhythm while we debate the best use of the money.

"Let's get some beer," Tom says.

I consider this. It is a good idea, but there is no way we are going to score alcohol. I can maybe get away with smokes, but no one is going to believe I am twenty-one. It is better to pretend it didn't matter, though, or they might not think I can get beer if I want to. "Ah, I don't feel like drinking. Besides, that's not enough to get us drunk, so why bother?"

"Yeah," Skeeter says. "If we can't get enough to get drunk, screw it."

Tom laughs. "Crap, Skeeter, one beer and you would be wasted."

"Would not," Skeeter says. "I could out-drink you any day of the week."

"Prove it, lightweight."

Skeeter stares hard at Tom. He gets that look in his eye, the one where he has decided the smallest kid in the class has to prove he is the toughest. That isn't good. I know what is going to happen next.

"Get us some beer, Devon."

"Skeeter, I told ya – I don't feel like drinking."

"I don't care. It's not for you. I gotta show this jerk who can drink the most."

"Yeah, come on, Devon." Tom smiles. "A twenty will get us a case, that's eleven each for you and me, and two for Skeeter."

"So you're a math whiz now, huh?" I try to blow it off but nothing can get Skeeter off course once he feels challenged. I spit out over the sidewalk. "Fine. Let's get some beer."

I have no clue where we are going to get the beer. Something would come up. Something always did. That's why the guys hung out with me; there was always something coming up.

I shove my hands into my pockets and cut across the street, Tom and Skeeter close behind. I can tell the bravado is wearing off Tom, he keeps looking to the side to see if Skeeter has calmed down. He hasn't.

"So, Devon, where we gonna get the beer?" Skeeter is fired up, anxious to prove his manhood.

"I don't know, man, we'll get some. Don't worry about it."

Tom tries to regain his courage. "Yeah, man, no worries. Devon is the man, he'll get us some brew."

I glance at Tom, see how nervous he was. Come to think of it, I don't think I have ever seen him drink. It's not like a couple fourteen year olds get beer that often. I've only been drunk three times in my life, and none of them were with Tom.

"You sure you feel like drinking today, Tom?" I ask. I know he wants an out, a way to avoid this. But life isn't about making it easy on everyone else. You have to look out for yourself, have to keep your position in the pecking order. And Tom, well, I peck at the top of his head everyday. As Tom looks over at Skeeter, Skeeter doesn't say anything, it is like he is ready to lay it down this time. That isn't going to happen. If I start to let these guys make their own decisions they might find someone else to hang with.

"You've never had a beer, have you?" There it was. The accusation that will put everyone back in line.

"Sure, sure I have. I've had plenty." His face turns red.

Skeeter jumps in. "Oh, you're lying. You don't even want us to find some beer, 'cause you know I'll out-drink you. You're a beer virgin!"

Tom shoves Skeeter, almost knocking the little guy over. I stepp in between them before they can start swinging.

"Hey, hey, knock it off. We'll settle this the right way. We'll get the beer and see who drinks the most."

"Yeah, fine," Tom says. "That's fine with me. I'll show the little squirt."

"Who you calling little?" Skeeter is in Tom's face.

I pull him back. "Enough, Skeeter. You can show him up later, with the beer, like I said."

I shrug my head, gesture toward the street. "Let's head down to Eighth Street. I got an idea on how to get some beer."

G anesh

I am working the counter at the Quickie Mart. Nothing unusual about that, I do it every day, seven days a week, three hundred and sixty-five days a year. After four years I got the day shift. Lucky me, I thought. Not so many crazies running around at three in the afternoon. I have been robbed seven times on the night shift. Two years on the day shift and nothing worse than shoplifters and the occasional fight among the narrow aisles. But no guns. That is what I am most glad of. No guns.

Three young punks come in, looking like they had no money and nothing but trouble to be getting into. I know their kind the moment they enter the store. I keep my eye on the video monitors and the three wide angle mirrors that allow me to carefully scrutinize the activity going on in my store. Yes, my store, even though some faceless corporation owns it, I have been here for six years and it is every bit my store as it is their store. It is not the corporation sweeping the dirt and cleaning the counters and making sure the syrup mixture is appropriate. No, it is my store, and I watch it like the hawk.

The three punks are going to be bad news, I can feel it in my heart. I know the kids in my neighborhood, the ones that come in here for gum or soda or comics. I know the good ones, and the bad ones, and even the bad ones are not truly all that bad. Once they learn that I watch their every move, that there is no getting away when Ganesh is seeing with the monitors and the mirrors, they learn to behave. But new kids, kids that did not know me or my store, they are always trouble.

It is easy to see the roles each play in their pack by the way they walk, the way they look to the kid carrying the skateboard for direction. The small one, that is the one that concerns me, that is the one that will do something stupid just to prove a point. The other boy is just that – a boy looking to fit in, he will run at the first sign of trouble. But the skateboard kid – if he holds in line then it will be okay. If he decides this is not the place to cause trouble, then the others will go quietly along.

"Hello and good afternoon to you, my fine young men. How can I help you today?"

The one with the skateboard answers for them, as I knew he would. "Oh, we're just looking around. No crime in that, is there?"

"Oh, certainly not, no crime in looking, my young friend."

The kids go down an aisle and pretend to read the magazines. They look for the girlie magazines but I do not stock those. Not in my store. Mrs. Cranston comes in for her daily lottery ticket and I try to talk with her while still keeping an eye on the mirrors.

"Hello, beautiful lady," I say.

"Oh, good afternoon, Ganesh. How are you today?"

I smile at her pronunciation – it sounds like she is calling me the garnish from a dinner salad, but I do not hold it against her. She is one of the few who bother to try – who do not refer to me as that Indian fellow or the foreigner running the Quickie Mart.

"I am just fine, Mrs. Cranston. The usual numbers?"

She nods, the wispy white hair struggling to hide her pink-white scalp, her watery eyes still bright blue. She is lovely, in her infirmity, this kindly old woman who stops in each afternoon to play the numbers of her late husband's birthday and their wedding anniversary. I punch in 3, 12, 6,

5 in the lottery machine for the daily Pick Four and hand her the ticket. She hands me a single dollar bill, crisp and clean, looking as if she ironed it before placing it in her purse and walking to my store.

The crash from the rear of the store takes my attention away from Mrs. Cranston. One of the boys – the small one – has fallen into the stacked display of Coca Cola cans. It had taken me three hours to stack them just right, in a pattern of a football field with goal posts. I rush from behind the counter to make sure the kid has not harmed himself, thoughts of lawsuits running through my mind.

A flash in the mirror as the door chimes and I turn to see the skateboard kid run out of the store, carrying a case of beer. I have fallen for the oldest game in the book. Ganesh, six year veteran of Quickie Mart tricks, has been fooled by a simple distraction con.

I turn around but of course the other kids are already running for the door and there is nothing I can do but bend over and pick up the Coca Cola cans and reassemble my football display.

Mrs. Cranston

I am waiting for my lottery ticket to print out. Ganesh seems distracted; he keeps looking around me and in those big gleaming mirrors that remind me of the silver punch bowls we had at our wedding reception. Oh, Momma was so proud of us, and Poppa spent every last dime he had giving Harold and me the best wedding the little town of Kanapolis had ever seen.

I see the reflection of the boys in the mirror. Boys like that, no wonder Ganesh is fretting. We didn't have boys like that in Kanapolis, not back then, anyway. Don't know why we ever moved to the city. This isn't a place to raise a family. Not that we ever had boys of our own to raise. The Good Lord must have decided that wasn't for us.

I take the ticket and pass Ganesh a one dollar bill. I glance down at the numbers. The dates instantly flash through my mind: March 12, 1923 and June 5, 1944. I try not to think of February 28, 1996, when Harold passed away, but I can't help it. But even if that day never leaves my mind, I won't use it to play the lottery. No, I wouldn't want to win with those numbers.

There's a crash from the back of the store. I turn around as Ganesh dashes from behind the counter to check on the boy who has knocked over the cans. I stare hard at the other one, the one with a case of beer under his hand who tosses a crumpled piece of paper at me as he runs out of the store. I surprise myself by catching it.

I hear Ganesh curse as the other two boys follow the first out of the store. He shakes his head and starts to pick up the cans and restack them. I unfold the paper to discover the boy may be taking beer but he wasn't stealing it. He had thrown a twenty dollar bill to me.

I look at Ganesh, his dark skin and oily hair shining as he stacks can after can to recreate his diorama. I look down at the twenty-dollar bill. I think about how Ganesh greets me every day with a smile. I think of how my numbers never come up. I open my purse and put the twenty in alongside the ticket.

"Goodbye, Ganesh. I will see you tomorrow."

He waves at me and I push open the door, the little bells on top jingling as I let it close behind me. Angels getting their wings, I think, another pair of wings for an angel with every ringing of the bell.

I place my hand over my knit hat to keep it in place as I walk along the cracked sidewalk. The wind is picking up. It is warm out but I still feel a chill in my bones. January or August hardly matters to me; I find myself donning hat, scarf and coat no matter what the month. I do add a pair of leather gloves in the coldest months.

I walk the three blocks to my apartment building. The few people I pass do little more than nod at me; most ignore me completely. Thirty years in the same neighborhood, and less than a dozen people from the Quickie Mart to my apartment know my name. It wasn't like that in Kanapolis. Back there – back then – people knew their neighbors. We were like a big extended family, from one side of town to the other. People cared about each other. People smiled and told you good afternoon and helped an old lady across the street. Now, I'm lucky to make it halfway across before the 'Don't Cross' starts flashing and at least a couple times a week the horns are honking before I reach the other side.

Freddie lets me into the building. Freddie is one of the dozen. He isn't the nicest person I know but since he is on that short list I smile anyway and thank him even when he only buzzes me in and doesn't hold the door open for me. I go to the elevator and push the call button.

The elevator creaks and whines. I pray my usual Hail Mary and it gets me up to the fourteenth floor in one piece. I shuffle down the dark hallway. One of these days I am going to buy a bunch of hundred watt bulbs and replace every one of the dim forty watt bulbs. It would give the landlord a heart attack to see his electric bill go up by fifty cents.

I fish the door key from my purse, pausing a moment when I see the twenty dollar bill sitting there beside the lottery ticket. I shake my head. I deserved it, the boy had thrown it to me. I go to that store every day, and my numbers never win. Besides, it wouldn't have changed anything. The boys were still committing a crime. Drinking beer at their age. Why, the first sip of alcohol I had was at my wedding reception. And after that, a glass of wine at Christmas dinner, maybe a glass of champagne on New Year's Eve. Certainly never beer, and not when I was a child.

I find the key and open the door. I close it behind me, sliding the deadbolt in place and attaching the security chain. Another reminder of where I live now, of how it is in the world today. We used to leave the door unlocked year round. It took us three days to find the house keys when we sold the little place on Carol Street, when we left Kanapolis for the big city where there were jobs to be had. I blink the tears aside. All the job had done was to take my Harold away from me for fifty hours a week. It had taken the country out of him, had soured his sweet nature until the last ten years had been nothing more than two people living out shallow, meaningless lives. Sharing the same eight hundred square feet of living space and not even communicating.

That doesn't matter, I tell myself. We loved each other. No matter how bad it got in the end, we loved each other. When the cancer finally took him, when I felt his hand go limp in mine at the hospital, I knew my love was gone forever. That until the Good Lord called me to His side, I would be alone. That was my cross, I decided. To be alone, without Harold, until it was my time.

I putter around the apartment, watering the plants, doing my daily dusting. I don't know where it comes from, but every day a thin film of dust manages to cover almost everything in the place. I suppose it is the dirt and grime from the city, finding its way in through the cracks of the building, Lord knows there are enough of those. I tape up blankets across the windows to keep out the cold wind in the winter.

By the time I finish dusting, it's almost time for the five o'clock drawing. I turn on the small television set that sits on the coffee table in front of the old sofa. It warms up and soon a fuzzy picture is displayed. I turn up the volume as the perky young announcer flips the switch and the balls start bouncing around in the lottery machine.

They do the Pick Three first. I try not to watch, as a couple times the three numbers were among the four I play in my game and that just irritated me so much I could have spit. I see the numbers anyway: fourteen, five, thirty-six. Hah, I would have wasted my dollar playing that game today. I bite my upper lip as she resets the machines and announces they will now draw the numbers for the Pick Four game.

A ping pong with the number three painted on it shoots into the selection tube. I remain calm. It is easy to match the first number. A twelve comes next and I feel my pulse quicken. When the six is drawn next, I am on the edge of the sofa. I am blinking to keep the tears from my eyes when the last ball shoots into the tube. I cannot see the number through my blurred vision but I hear the young woman announce five as the final number.

I sit back in the sofa, trying to hear her voice as she repeats the numbers. The blood is pounding in my head but I still make out the numbers as she repeats them: three, twelve, six and five. All four numbers, all in the right order.

Oh, Harold, I think. Oh Harold, thank you. I get up, trembling. I panic when I do not see my purse on the little table by the door, then I remember I set it on the kitchen counter. I walk into the small kitchen and breathe a sigh of relief when I see the black leather purse just where I left it.

I decide I should have something to eat, as I am feeling rather light headed now. I make some toast and spread a thin layer of peanut butter on the dry bread. It settles my stomach down. I wash the plate and knife, dry them and put them back away.

I smile as I pick up the purse. I walk to the door and remove the security chain, slide the deadbolt free, and head back out to buy some hundred watt bulbs.

F reddie

I'm reading the sports section in the Tribune when the old lady comes down. Mrs. Cranston, she's been living here since before I was born. Gives me a crummy fruit cake at Christmas, hard as a rock. Still, there's worse people here. At least she won't give me a hard time. Buzz her in once or twice a day, she never has anything too heavy for her to carry so she doesn't treat me like her hired hand, not like Mrs. Johnson does. That old bat makes me carry her groceries up once a week. And not even a Christmas card from the Johnson's.

"Going out again?" I ask. She doesn't usually go out in the evening. And never at night. Still, I guess it won't be dark for a couple hours yet.

She smiles at me and nods. She looks more alive than usual, like she's... happy, I guess. "I'll buzz you in when you get back, then." I turn back to the paper.

A quiet "ahem" makes me look back up and I see Mrs. Cranston standing in front of the counter. Great, she must need me to carry something. Probably bought a new chair, something that's going to put my back out. "You need something, Mrs. Cranston?"

She opens up her purse and fumbles around in it.

"I got a master key, I can let you in if you need me to," I offer.

She shakes her head. "No, Freddie, I don't need that. I just wanted to thank you for buzzing me in all the time. You never make me wait when it's raining or cold outside. I appreciate that."

Then she pulls a twenty dollar bill out of her old lady purse and places it on the counter, smoothing out the wrinkles with her spotted, thin hands. "This is for you."

"Geez, thanks Mrs. Cranston. But you don't have to do that, it's my job to let you in." The words come out naturally, but inside I am thinking that maybe this makes up for that fruit cake and please don't believe me, lady, please don't take it back.

She purses her lips and places a finger on the bill and I think I blew it, she is going to put it back in that old lady purse and I probably won't even get the crummy fruit cake this year. But instead she pushes the twenty toward me and says, "I want you to have it, Freddie. It's not for me, not anymore."

I shake my head at the strange comment but slowly reach down and pick up the money. She smiles at me; her eyes are bright but brimming with tears. She closes her purse and turns around and slowly walks out of the building.

I place the twenty dollar bill in my shirt pocket. Crazy old lady. I turn back to the sports section and finish reading the paper while I wait for the end of my shift.

Half an hour later I am heading down to Mugsy's Saloon. God knows I can use a drink after sitting on my butt all day. I don't know what else to do, not since Wendy left with the kids. Like she was a whole lot of fun anyway. Always complaining about money, about me not helping with the housework when I'm out earning our room and board six days a week. Good riddance to her, that's what I say.

I walk the six blocks to Mugsy's with my hands shoved in my pockets. It was chilly for this time of the year, and I wished I had a jacket. Oh well, Mugsy's would be warm. He always had it set to eighty degrees there, said the warmer the room the better the cold beer tasted. Darn if he wasn't right, it always went down smooth.

I open the door and the heat hits me square in the face. God, it felt good. I take a quick look around to see who's sitting in the four narrow booths that line one side of the bar. A couple I haven't seen before are in the closest one, a pretty blonde with some guy that looks like he sells cars. I turn away and look at the dozen stools on the outside of the long bar. Joe and Kevin, regulars, are sitting there, along with a few more strangers. I head for the empty stool next to Joe and sit down.

"Evening, gents," I say.

"Hey, Freddie, how's it going?" Joe asks.

"Oh, same old, same old," I say. I lean forward and nod at Kevin, sitting on the other side of Joe. "What's up, Kevin?"

"A direction away from the gravitational center of a celestial body," Kevin answers. He grins widely.

Joe and I groan at the old line, one we have heard Kevin use a million times. But it wouldn't be the same if I didn't ask him, and it wouldn't be the same if he hadn't answered. It was important for things to be the same, to have a comfortable, familiar place like Mugsy's where things didn't get turned upside down without notice. A place where people didn't pull up and leave you hanging without even telling you things were messed up.

Mugsy saunters over with an open Bud Lite and slides it to me. I thank him and he moves on back to the strangers sitting at the opposite end of the bar. He's schmoozing the rich ones, the new people, knowing they are going to drop more money in an hour on expensive vodka cocktails and five dollar cigars than Joe, Kevin and I will spend in a week. That's okay, we know how it is, what

Mugsy has to do to keep the place running so we can come in on a dead Tuesday night and have our couple of beers.

I take a long pull on the Bud Lite. "Man, it's been a day."

Joe nods. "I heard that, man. I heard that." He gestures with his head back to the opposite side of the bar. "Check this guy out, Freddie."

I turn my head around and see one of the rich guys stumbling our way. I turn back to Joe as the guy makes his way past us and to the bathroom. "Man, he's lit."

"I heard them talking about wanting to play cards, before you got here. They're looking for a game."

I glance over at the three guys drinking their eight dollar drinks. "The rest just as drunk?"

Joe shrugs. "They sure ain't sober."

I think about winning a couple hundred dollars off the suits. Sure would be nice. I could get something real pretty for Maggie's birthday next month. Not that I have to, it was Wendy who took her away – I'm not responsible for child care payments. No, I don't have to do anything for her. But it would be nice.

"I'm up for it."

"Cool."

The next time Mugsy comes over to check on us we get him to let us use the room in back. Joe talks to the suits and we all head there, Joe, Kevin and I walking a whole lot straighter than the rich guys. Going to get Maggie a real nice present, I think. Going to be Daddy's girl again, I'll show Wendy she can't change things just like that.

H^{ugh}

Sometimes people need to be taught a lesson, to be put in their place. It isn't from any sense of malice, or even enjoyment – it is just the way life works. A shark doesn't feed from any desire to hurt its prey; it is merely being true to its nature.

Take these blue collar guys at the bar. They do their eight hours and punch out, and they come to have a beer and drink away their worries. That is natural, it is part of who they are. I don't blame them for that, I don't think less of them for playing their role in society. Likewise, I feel no remorse for acting my part.

Four watered-down drinks do nothing but take the edge off. I stumble along the hallway to their back room, knowing before I get there what I will see: boxes filled with empty beer bottles stacked high, a naked hundred watt bulb swinging above, a beat-up table with cigarette burn marks in the torn covering. Ah yes, the hard metal folding chairs, that completes the picture.

I lean heavily on a chair and pretend it keeps me from falling down. I lurch into it and scrape it noisily along the hard floor as I scoot closer to the table. We sit down, cautiously interspersing the locals with the newcomers in an every-other-chair pattern. I give a quick smirk to Greg and Thomas. They are legitimately drunk, but that is no matter. They know my game; even wasted, they know enough to carry things out. They may mess up a few hands for me in their exuberance, but in the end the cards will go my way. They always do, it is how the world works.

So two hours later, Greg is slumped back in his chair, his two hundred dollars split between two of the locals – Joe and Freddie, I believe they are called. The other local lost fifty bucks betting Aces against my two pair and headed out cursing, just half an hour after we sat down.

I know exactly how much money is sitting in front of each of us. I have a pretty good idea how much more lines the pockets of the two locals. I discount Thomas. He is sitting there quietly playing just a little behind, folding most hands. He is here as a foil, should I need a raiser, nothing more. Joe is the more experienced player, knowing when to hold and when to fold, but the way he holds his cards is a dead giveaway.

Three hands later I know he is sitting on three of a kind and my flush drains him dry. He bites his lip and for a moment I think about the gun in my pocket, but then he sits back and nods his head. He knows I did not cheat. He doesn't know I had him read all the way; he thinks he just got unlucky, one very good hand running into a monster hand. That's why he'll lose the next time he plays against someone like me. It's also why he'll keep winning in his local game.

I look at my watch. Almost time to head out. I give Thomas the signal. He raises big the next hand. Freddie folds. I call him. Thomas draws two cards, I take three. He pushes his money into the pot. I raise him. He sighs heavily, reaches into his wallet and drops his last fifty on the pile. "Call."

I show my two pair and Thomas mucks his cards face down into the deck. "I'm tapped."

"Sorry, old boy." I quickly gather the cards, pretty certain that Thomas had me beat, but he knows who can finish the game with the best chance. "Looks like it's just you and me, Freddie."

"Deal them," Freddie says.

It takes five hands before I have him ready for the final blow. I make a final raise, sitting on a straight, thanks to some fancy dealing. He has three of a kind. He empties his wallet, then with a slight hesitation digs into his shirt pocket and drops another twenty on top.

The blood is in the water, there is nothing this poor man can do to prevent the killing. I lay the four-five-six-seven-eight down on the table and I see the light fade from his eyes. He had hopes of changing his life, from a simple poker game in the back of a bar, but that isn't how it works. I had to take his money. I had to do what comes natural.

"Good game, gentleman," I say. "Better luck next time."

Another man, another night, and those words might have resulted in the brawl I thought could have occurred when Joe lost earlier. But Freddie is a beaten man. He has no fight left in him.

Thomas and I half-carry Greg back out to the bar. I order a round of drinks for the locals and have the bartender call us a cab.

M^{iles}

I'm a little surprised to see the three dudes all dressed up coming out of Mugsy's. When Mugsy called me I figured it was to take someone home from the neighborhood, someone too drunk to walk three blocks on their own. These guys are not typical customers for Mugsy's.

The three of them crowd into the back seat, two of them propping the third one up against the left side door. The blonde haired one slams the door shut.

I check him out in the rearview mirror. His eyes lock onto mine and it's like the guy is trying to read my mind. I shake off the thought. "Where you guys heading?"

"Downtown," he answers.

I shrug at the non-specific answer. They have money – he does anyway, I can tell that. I'm happy to drive around in circles as long as the meter is running.

I shift into drive and pull away from the side of the street, easing into traffic. The back seat is quiet. I glance in the mirror and every time the eyes of the blonde-haired man meet mine. I clear my throat but the usual patter runs dry and after a couple halting efforts I let the silence hang heavy in the cab.

I check in with dispatch and it seems like the man is trying to decipher a code from the brief staccato sentences I rasp into the mike, I feel him listening in from the back seat. I repeat my location and general direction for dispatch. Louis answers back with a "I got it the first time, Miles, give me a freakin' break," but I don't care, my nerves are acting up and I don't trust this ride.

I drive slower than usual. When I get nervous I take it easy, making sure not to get in an accident or miss a turn.

If you have a bad ride, one that is spooking you, you want to drive super fast and get it over with, but if you start doing that then they get nervous and the tension just feeds on it and before you know it you got some crazy guy pulling a knife at you screaming that you're taking the long way and screwing them on the fare.

The guy slouched against the left side door starts moving around. I glance his way in the mirror. He is rubbing his hands through his hair, loosening his tie. Not good, this guy is in bad shape. I flick my eyes to the other side and blonde hair is staring straight into my mind again.

I call in the cross streets to Louis again and dial the volume down before he replies. I clear my throat. "Getting close to the bypass. Which way do you want me to take?"

The drunk guy has rolled the window down, trying to get fresh air, so I miss whatever blonde hair said. "I'm sorry, I didn't catch that."

He stares at me like it's my fault his friend prevented me from hearing his words. The ramp is approaching. He doesn't say anything and I stay on the avenue.

"This way is fine. We're almost there."

I nod and slow down a bit more, just in case he tells me to stop at the last moment. A man in a Cadillac honks and gives me the finger as he swerves around me. I ignore him. If I had a dollar for every time someone flipped me the bird, I sure as heck wouldn't be driving a cab.

I glance in the mirror. The drunk guy is swallowing every couple seconds. I pray the stop is coming up soon. It is not soon enough, however.

"I'm going to puke," the drunk guy says.

"Just hold on," the guy in the middle says. "We're almost there."

I start pulling to the curb as soon as I see the drunk's hand go up to cover his mouth. "Out the window, out the window!" the middle guy yells, and then this drunk moron, this idiot, rolls the window up and pukes straight into the glass.

I slam the cab to a stop. I jump out, yank the rear door open. "Get out, get out of my cab before I call the police on you!"

At those words the blonde hair man shoves his hand in his coat pocket. I see the bulge there, but even knowing a gun is waiting to be drawn out does not quell my anger at having this drunk vomit in my back seat.

"Easy, easy does it, Miles."

Hearing my name come from his mouth does what the presence of a gun did not, and the anger dissolves in an icy wave of fear. But I am still upset. "He puked in my car, man! I won't be able to take another fare till I clean this mess up." I try to stay calm, to remain indignant, as a shield against the man's stare, a barrier to protect me from his voice.

"Okay, I can understand you're upset. Tell you what, we'll go ahead and walk the last two blocks." He slides out the other side, avoiding the puke, and his buddies get out as well.

The man crosses behind the cab and over to me. He reaches into his pocket and I tense, ready to duck, ready to flee for my life. He pulls out a wad of bills and peels off two fifty dollar bills. "That's for the mess. Sorry."

I take the money, force myself to meet his eyes. "Meter is eighteen dollars, sir."

He freezes for a second, then laughs. He takes a twenty off the roll and hands it to me. "Keep the change."

The men walk away, the drunk one held up by the other two. I get back in the cab. The noxious smell hits me as soon as I sit down and I roll the front windows down. I head for the car wash on Martin Avenue. No attendants there, no one to yell at me for using their car vacuum on the back seat. I'll feel sorry for whoever uses it after me, but what can you do? It's not like I wanted anyone to puke in my cab. Not even for a hundred dollar tip. Hundred and twenty, I remind myself. As far as Louis knows, those dudes beat it as soon as I pulled over and stiffed me on the fare.

A couple people wave at me as I drive by but I have the service light off. They may not expect to ride in style in this neighborhood, but even around here crawling into a cab with a mess in the backseat is not going to go over. I try to breathe in through my mouth to avoid smelling it.

The tension is gone, the spookiness has left, and I am flying through the streets now. With instinct and habit I avoid the car doors opening, the cars changing lanes without signaling, the streets with traffic cops patrolling for offenders. A couple turns, a couple miserable lights that caught me and left me thanking the wind for blowing the smell out as the car stood still, and I arrive at the car wash.

I check my ashtray and only find a couple dollar's worth of quarters. I walk over to the change machine and curse when I see it is out of service. Great. It will take close to ten dollars to clean the back seat out. I know, I have done it dozens of times.

There is a Shell gas station down the street, on the corner of Eighth and Martin. I get back in the cab and drive over. The radio crackles, it is Louis, wondering where I am.

"Sorry, Louis, the last ride bailed on me. Drunk puked in the back seat, I'm at the car wash on Martin, have to clean it up."

"Miles, you come in short again and we're going to have to have a talk."

"Dude, it's not my fault. You sent me to that call, it's not like I picked them out myself. The guy puked, I pulled over, they ran on me. I sure wasn't going to leave the cab running to chase them down."

The radio crackles, and I wait for Louis' response. "Well, all I'm saying is you been short three out of the last four nights, Miles. Can't have that. One call ain't going to change what's been going on. You gotta bust it out, man."

I thumb the mike, ready to respond with a whole lot of attitude, but release the trigger before I do so. Louis is right, I haven't been pulling in a lot. And mostly it's been my choice. Those three nights I was short, I know why. It's not because I'm taking money off the top, or picking up people without turning the meter on. It's because I have to escape. Sometimes I just have to get out of this cab and ride in another world.

I thumb the mike again. "Okay, Louis, I hear you. I'll be in later."

I top the gas tank off and talk the attendant into selling me a ten dollar roll of quarters. I hand her a twenty, pocket the change next to the fifties.

S usie

God I hate my job. Sitting here watching people pull up, stick their card in the automated pumps and drive off. The only reason they have me here is in case something screws up, and believe me, if that happens I am going to care a whole lot more about keeping my butt from going up in flames than saving the gas station.

I'm glad the station doesn't sell beer. Bad enough, the drunks we get coming in here looking for a place to pee or a pack of cigarettes. If we sold beer by the quart this place would be a zoo. Too many bars around here, they would all come here for the cheaper beer or after last call.

Of course, without beer sales and with pay at the pump, it's pretty boring around here. Not that I want the drunks, but God, if we had something other than pop and pork rinds maybe people would come in and buy something instead of zooming off without a second thought that I need somebody to talk to.

There're some regulars that do stop in, that apparently have cast iron stomachs because they use the refillable sixty-four ounce traveling mug every day of the week. That stuff will tear you apart. Premium coffee, that's what the cardboard sign that fell behind the coffee pot said. Yeah, right. The sign cost more than what they paid for those beans.

Al, the owner, came by last week. He started talking about putting a hot dog machine in. As if hot dogs that are all wrinkled up from baking in the heat lamp for twelve hours are going to bring the customers in. I told him it was a great idea because he wants to hear that crap. Thinks I look up to him. If brown nosing a little keeps me employed then

I'll flatter Al a little. I caught him checking me out. Not that I'm anything special, but he's forty, bald and fat, so anything that weighs less than him, is half his age and doesn't need to hide in public is a goddess to him. Of course he'll never get anywhere, I'm not that desperate. But a little flattery, a little longer I keep the job. It doesn't hurt anyone.

A cab pulls up next to pump four. I check out the security camera. He lifts the handle and flips the pump on. Cabbies are okay, they pay in cash. Usually pretty talkative, conversation to relieve the boredom. I turn the pump on and give him the go ahead over the speaker system.

He comes in five minutes later. He's kind of cute. Dark skinned, wearing a beat up leather jacket that suits him. You could pick him out of a lineup as a cab driver.

"Hey, there, how you doing tonight?"

I shrug. "I'm here, it can't be all that good."

"Ah, hey, could be worse. At least nobody's throwing up in your place of business."

I crinkle my nose in disgust at the thought. "I've had it happen. Not too often, probably not as many times as you. Man, why can't people control themselves? I can't imagine putting myself through that."

He nods. "I hear you. Say, how about helping me out? My cab is a mess. The change machine is broken down at the car wash – can you sell me a roll of quarters?"

I look at him. He seems nice, he seems like someone I should know, someone who should come in here every day – not for a toxic sixty-four ounces of coffee, but because he wants to talk to me, to share his stories of passengers he picked up, maybe a famous actor or a writer or even the drunks who got sick in his back seat. He hands me a twenty and I ring up the six odd bucks for the gas. I pull out a roll of quarters from the cash drawer. "Here you go," I say.

He smiles. Our hands connect for a minute and I feel his warmth seep into my finger tips, then the contact is lost and he is waiting for his change. I pass over three bucks and a handful of coins and then with a wave and a final thanks he goes out the door, gets into his cab and drives off.

It happens every couple of weeks. I shouldn't be upset. There are a million – well, a thousand – nice guys out there. I meet them in my little gas station, and for twelve or thirteen seconds I think that this is the guy that will feel the little spark of electricity and hesitate ever so slightly at the door before looking back over his shoulder and asking if I would like to go get a drink. Or watch a movie. Or go for a walk.

But as of today, this has not occurred. As of today, the only hesitation is when they try to remember if they got everything, which is funny since other than cigarettes and pork rinds the pickings are pretty slim. No glance over the shoulder, no bashful reddening of their face as they try to work up their nerve to ask me out. Nothing. Nothing, nothing, nothing. Maybe the hot dog machine will help.

Another car pulls in. I don't recognize the car or the driver. He slides the pump on. I don't have the same feeling with most strangers as I do with cabbies, and I turn the speaker on and tell him the pumps are pre-pay after six o'clock. He frowns, shakes his head like I make the rules – which I sort of do, on my shift anyway but it says right on the pump that they are pre-pay – and slowly walks into the store.

He takes out a hundred dollar bill and places it on the counter. "That cover it?" he asks.

I want to answer sarcastically but nothing comes to mind so I just place the bill on top of the pump readouts and say, "Yeah."

He walks out and I start wondering what would happen if he glanced back, if he gave me a smile instead of a smirk and asked if I felt like going for a drink, or a dance, or a drive along the highway to some unlighted parking lot where we would make out like a couple of high school kids. I shake my head when the buzzer sounds. He's back at the pump, waiting for me to turn it on. I flip the switch and watch as he smolders alongside his car, waiting for his anger to ignite the fumes escaping from the open tank.

He comes back in and I count out seventy-four dollars and eleven cents in change. I try a weak "Have a nice day" to make up for daydreaming while he was waiting for me to turn the pump on but he sneers at me and I don't think I wanted to go out with him anyway.

D onald

I flip the handle back and forth. A crackling noise comes from overhead and I hear some girl tell me I have to pay first. Like I looked as if I would run off without paying. Nothing to do about it, running on fumes now and have no clue where the next gas station is. I go through the door and see a scrawny white chick, couldn't be more than twenty years old. This little girl trying to show me up? As if.

I show her a hundred dollar bill. Yeah, that's right girl, old Donald has some scratch on him. Different story when you see Ben Franklin smiling at you from a C note, isn't it?

I head back out to the car. After a minute of standing there I see the stupid girl is just sitting there, staring off into space. I slam my palm against the buzzer and see her jerk to awareness. The pump kicks on and I stand there, cooling off, trying not to let the little girl get under my skin.

After squeezing another couple squirts into the tank – forget that no topping off nonsense, I'm filling it to the brim when I gas up – I head back in and she gives me my change. She tries to make nice, now that she sees old Donald is loaded, but I wouldn't waste a minute of my time on her scrawny butt. I give her a look of disdain before stuffing the bills into my pocket, letting her know that seventy-some bucks is just small change for old Donald.

The heck with her, the heck with all the skinny white chicks who don't have enough on them to hold on to. They don't care about old Donald, why should I care about them. Going to find me somebody who knows a good thing when it walks into the room. Who recognizes old Donald has it going on. Somebody who'll show old Donald a good time.

But before I find a lady I got to replace that C note. I head down to Smitty's Barbershop. I got a hot tip on the Northwestern game. Starting running back caught a hard shot to the thigh in practice yesterday. Line is three and a half, I figure without him they're going to lose by more than that.

I park the car and walk up to the shop. Walt is leaning against the red brick wall, holding court with a couple of the younger boys from the neighborhood. I nod at him, he nods back. We respect each other, but neither of us admits it. We just won't talk trash, won't put the other in a spot where it comes down to anything serious. We've known each other too long for that.

I push open the door and see Trevor styling away behind his chair. I grab a newspaper and sit down on the bench. There's a couple guys I recognize, we shoot the usual bull back and forth while I wait my turn.

A little bit later I am in the chair. "Give me a real close shave, Trevor. I'm going to find me a woman tonight."

Trevor chuckles, his deep baritone voice booms out. "Sure thing, Donald, I'll make you so pretty you'll be beating them ladies off with a baseball bat." He lathers my face up, the warm cream feeling good against my worn skin.

In between swipes we have our usual conversation. He asks about my Momma, I check on his wife and kids. And I casually ask him what the line is on the Northwestern game.

"Oh, I don't know, Donald. I suppose I would call it three and a half." His voice is softer, talking about business now, but I feel the bass reverberating in my ears, as he leans in close to discuss the details.

"Well, now, I wouldn't mind taking Iowa, and giving you those points," I tell him.

Trevor wipes the blade clean on his towel and does a final cut across my cheek. He rubs my face clean with the towel, and I reach a hand across it, dragging my fingers both ways and not feeling a hint of stubble.

"Mighty fine, Trevor, mighty fine."

"Thank you Donald, I aim to please." He lowers his voice. "How much?"

I show three fingers.

"Three hundred?"

"Thousand," I tell him.

He whistles softly. "I can't cover that, Donald. Not unless you pay up front."

I smile. "That's fine, Trevor. Old Donald, he's good for it." I open up my wallet and grab the thick sheaf of bills out and hand them to the barber. "Three grand, my man."

Trevor quickly counts the bills. "You sure about this, Donald? It's a lot of money to put on a three and a half point toss up."

I clap him on the shoulder. "I got a feeling, buddy. Place it for me, okay?"

"If that's what you want."

I reach into my pocket and pull out the crumpled wad. I extract one twenty and hand it to Trevor. "Here, thanks for the shave. Now I gotta head out and find that woman."

Trevor

Old Donald, he's all right. I have no idea where that brother got the three grand, but that's his business, I guess. I put the bills in my right pocket, the twenty dollar tip in my left. I ain't going to mix the money up, no, that's the sure fire way to end up on the wrong end of this here razor.

I tell Jerome to take over the chair and go into the back room. I call up Mister Watts, tell him I got three extra-large on Iowa with the points. I reassure him I got the bet money up front, that it's Donald placing the bet, and he tells me I did good. I 'yes, sir' and thank him and do all the butt-kissing I have to in order to keep on his good side. These knees, they don't need any baseball bats alongside them, that's for sure.

I hang up and wonder again how Donald got the money. And why he was willing to put it all on Iowa. I think about the twelve hundred I got stashed in the wall behind the heat vent. I think about how much better twenty-four hundred would be.

I pace back and forth. Man, that would be something, an extra twelve hundred bucks, would make things a lot easier. I could even take a little three day vacation, go visit my sister in Atlanta, buy her and the nephews something nice to remember me by. It's been close to three years since I seen them. It sure would be nice.

I decide to do it. I pick up the phone and call Mister Watts back up.

"Mister Watts, I got another guy — just came in, wants to bet on the Iowa — Northwestern game. Is the line still three and a half?"

"Yeah, sure, that's it. How much?"

I quickly think about what is in the register now, and what I got in the bank. I am sweating, my voice seems weak to me as I tell him. "Two extra-large, sir."

"Lot of action today. You got the money?"

I hesitate. I don't, I know I don't but I feel the blood racing through my veins and I swallow hard, replying, "Yeah, Mister Watts, I got the money."

"Cool. Who's he want?"

"What?"

"The bet. Who's he taking, Iowa or Northwestern?"

Donald placed three grand on Iowa. Donald, the man who hardly ever bets more than a couple hundred, the man who was all smiles with a clean shave and out looking for girls. He seemed like it was a sure thing. Like he knew something. But still, it was Donald.

"Northwestern. The man wants Northwestern and the points."

"Got it."

I hang up and suddenly my legs are giving out on me. I stumble over to a chair and sit down, mopping the sweat from my forehead, trying to calm down. What have I done? My life hangs on a bunch of kids tossing a football around.

Jerome comes in ten minutes later; I am still sitting in the chair, staring vacantly at the wall, trying to figure out why on earth I did this, what made me make this foolish leap today. I have no answers for myself or for him when he asks if anything is wrong.

I shake my head and get up. "People waiting?"

He nods. "Couple. I cut a few, but Henry won't let me do his. Keeps saying he'll wait for you."

"Okay. Tell him I'll be out in a minute." I head to the bathroom and wash off the sweat. I dry off and go out to cut Henry's hair.

Jerome

I give Gee a real good cut, sharp as a razor. I watch him admire his reflection, see how tight my lines are, how the lines stand out. It's the best haircut the man ever got and he knows it.

Gee does a real slow nod as he checks it out. He winks at me. "Nice job, Jerome."

"Thanks, Gee."

I take the sheet off him and let the small bits of hair fall onto the floor. Gee gets up, hands me a ten for the cut. He is about to put the wallet back in his jeans when he stops and opens it back up.

"Oh, no, man you don't got to tip me."

Gee laughs, pulls a card out from the worn brown billfold. "It's not exactly a tip, Jerome." He hands me the card. "Meet me there at ten. Don't be late."

"Ten. Tonight. Sure thing, Gee. I'll be there."

He winks, his trademark sign. "Cool."

It isn't until after he leaves that I actually read what is on the card. It's from a dance club. A real hot dance club, one that would never let me past the bouncer. Jerome, with your sharp little scissors, you just got your foot in the door.

The next couple hours crawl by. I don't mind old Henry Johnson telling me he'd rather wait than let a young punk like me cut his hair. Let Trevor have him, he's half bald anyway, not much to do with that head but shave it all off and pretend you went bald on purpose.

I get a couple more cuts in, but mostly it's reading the paper and listening to the old guys talk. You would think they were all super-heroes from their stories. If there was a march, or a rally, or some bus going up in flames, they were there. Even if half of it happened five states away from where they were at the time. They keep telling me I got no sense of history, no respect for my elders, no appreciation for what they went through to give me the life I have now. Yeah, some life, cutting hair for two dollar tips and a few bucks an hour. Thanks, Pops, for saving the black people. Oh, you weren't in chains? You were doing the same thing I'm doing, no better, no worse? Yeah, that's what I thought.

Finally nine o'clock comes. I mosey up to Trevor. I can tell he's got me read, that he knows what's coming.

"You want another advance, don't you?"

"It's just until Friday. Come on, I did a lot of cuts yesterday, some more today. Can you give me fifty?"

"Boy, don't you know you're just pouring your money down the drain? You go spending it on a Wednesday night, you won't have nothing come the week-end. And don't think you can touch me up for more on Friday, no sir, that ain't going to happen."

"Please, Trevor, can I just have it? It's important, I got something to do tonight."

His eyes narrow and he stares hard. "It's with that Gee, isn't it? What did I tell you about him, Jerome? That boy is trouble with a capital T. You just keep working hard, someday you'll have your own chair." His voice softens. "Someday you can have this whole place, you keep at it like you been doing."

"You think this is what I want to do with my life? You think I want to spend twelve hours a day listening to a bunch of old farts talk about how they changed the world? You're crazy. I got better things to do. Bigger things. I'm not going to settle for clipping hair for ten bucks a cut."

Trevor stiffens. I have gone too far, for a moment I think he is going to hit me. He must have seen me flinch because he again relaxes. His voice is low, low and painful.

"You think I settled? You think this barbershop, this business, that I built from nothing was settling? Let me tell you this, I ain't settled for a thing in my life. I worked hard, and I'm proud of this place. Settling would have been tipping back the bottle or smoking grass instead of busting my butt to create something nice in my neighborhood. A safe place, a good place, where people can come in and talk without worrying about guns or drugs or cops brow beating you for walking outside at night."

He pulls out some bills from his left pocket. He takes three twenties and shoves them at my chest. "There, go on with your important business. Me, I got floors to sweep."

My mouth is dry. I have no response for this man who has treated me like a son. It isn't fair, I think, I want to tell him it isn't fair. I didn't mean to hurt him, but couldn't he see how it was? Man, Gee comes by driving his fancy convertible and his gold chains, flashing wads of cash. Why wouldn't I want that life? Why wouldn't I want easy money, women fighting over me, all for a little business in the alleys and not a bit of sweeping up hair clippings?

I take a glance around the barbershop. I shake my head. The door bells ring as I let myself out and walk down the street to my apartment.

I feel relief when I find the place empty. Good, Momma's not home yet. I sure don't feel like arguing with her about going out, not after hearing the lecture from Trevor. I take a quick shower and dress in my best clothes. This is your chance, Jerome, this is it. You get in good tonight, and no more worries. You can move Momma to a nicer place, you can have more than one set of clothes that you can go to the clubs in. It's all going to happen, if you can make it work tonight.

I splash on some extra cologne. I look in the mirror, adjust my collar. Yes, sir, Jerome, you are one mighty fine looking young man. I leave a note for Momma, telling her I will be home late. She'll be mad, but better mad than worried sick about why I'm not home. She'd be all worrying about me not wearing clean underwear and the people in the hospital seeing that when they bring me in from the horrible accident that I am in every time she doesn't know where I am at.

It's nine-thirty. I debate walking, but not sure I would make it without jogging, and extra-cologne or not, I don't want to show up sweaty and smelly. I go outside and get a cab, a lucky break in this neighborhood, and I am starting to think it will all be okay.

The cabbie drops me off. After paying him, I am down to seventy-five dollars, counting the money Trevor gave me and my tips today. As long as I don't have to buy more than a couple rounds, should be enough.

The line is short. The club doesn't really get going until after eleven. A couple hotties in front of me get let right in. I walk up, flashing my best smile, looking like the finest cat in the neighborhood. I make a move toward the door.

The bouncer puts out a thick forearm. "Where do you think you're going?"

I force the smile to remain. "Inside, my good man. I'm meeting someone."

His arm remains outstretched, blocking the entrance. "I don't know, my good man," he says, the words dripping with sarcasm. "I think my quota of single black men with no street cred is all used up tonight."

My smile leaves. I want to get up in his face, to call him out, but the thought of sweeping floors, of leaving Momma in that crummy apartment, of losing my opportunity, allows me to refocus and keep my cool. I laugh instead, and I see I catch him off guard, that he was expecting me to get upset. I press the advantage. "Come on now, big guy. It's early, the place isn't half-full yet. I'm here in my best threads, I have a little bit of money to spend in there, and then I'm gone for the night. All I'll be doing is buying some of those pretty ladies a drink or two, have my meeting with an old friend, and then I'm done. No skin off your back, my brother."

He looks at me. After a moment, he shrugs. I start forward again but his arm still blocks the way. I look down at it, then back up at him.

He puts his other hand out. "Twenty bucks."

"Excuse me?"

"Twenty bucks. Door fee."

I think about brushing this request off, but don't think it would work. He has nothing to lose, I have everything to gain. I give him a twenty dollar bill and hope that fifty bucks will get me through the meeting with Gee.

D arrell

Man, I'm sweating. Must be eighty degrees out here, and me stuck in this suit jacket. Boss man says he wants the place to look classy, so he makes me wear a suit that costs as much as I make in a week. At least he paid for it. Boss man, he's loaded. He doesn't care if this place makes money, as long as it looks like it does.

Getting towards ten o'clock. Still early. Couple people drift in. I stonewall a few of them, just because I can. If they were important, I'd know who they were. Or they wouldn't be showing up until midnight, when the place starts to hop. Just the hopefuls show up before then, the ones trying to slide in and make it until the cool people show up, so they can pretend they belong.

Course these girls walking up now, they belong pretty much anywhere they want to show those tight little bodies. I play the tough guy, give them the slow glance over as they walk up. Two blondes, could pass for sisters, and a brunette.

"Names?" I suck my gut in, my chest out, act like they aren't an automatic pass.

The brunette puts her hand on my chest, rubs it in a circle. "Aw, come on big fella, just be a good sport and pass us on in. You know the place will only look better with us decorating it."

The blondes giggle as I try to act tough. I jerk my head. "Go on."

The brunette leans in and gives me a kiss on the cheek, then slaps my butt. "Thanks, big fella. Maybe we'll see you on our way out."

I rub the lipstick off my cheek as I watch them strut on into the club. Man oh man, what I wouldn't give to be in there with them. Instead I get to stand out here for six hours getting sweaty and sore and trying to keep riff raff like me from walking in to spoil the scenery.

A young man comes up next in line. He's looking all flashy but I can tell those clothes have been worn more than once. I can tell this isn't his club. I stick my arm out as he tries to slide in behind the women.

He tries to smooth talk his way, but his uneven patter doesn't work on me. I can read him like a book. Heck, it was me, five years ago, thinking all I needed was to mix with the rich people and they would bring me in. A little drinking and dancing with the fast crowd and I would be on easy street. I'm on the street all right, standing up all night keeping watch on their little playground.

Still, it's not this kid's fault. It's not going to hurt anyone to let him have his dream for a night, to let him pretend he's moving on up to the big time. Can't get too sentimental, though – don't want anyone to think I'm a soft touch. I hit him up for twenty bucks before letting him slide by and enter the club.

It stays slow for another hour or so, a trickle of people coming in groups of three or four. Come midnight it starts to back up. No more free passes for young single black men pretending to belong. No, now it's Rolex and Armani, spandex and thirty-eight double dees, or back of the line, stay behind the rope for you.

I get a few more rub downs from young, and sometimes old, women, but no one like the brunette. I keep thinking about her, about how her hand felt, how her lips brushed against my cheek. She seemed real, like someone you could talk to, someone you could just sit down next to on the couch for three hours because she understood you were on your feet for six straight hours wearing a stupid jacket and were too tired to do anything else.

About two o'clock in the morning the line starts getting short again. Last call is at two, though people will keep coming until we lock the doors at four a.m. The flow reverses around three, three-thirty, then my job is as much making sure none of the drunks lie down on the street or get into a fight outside the place. I've got cabs lined up from two o'clock on, these people don't drive themselves, thank God, after all the alcohol they pour down their throats, and who knows what else they're swallowing or snorting in there.

The faces all blend together, I have no idea who has gone in and who has left. There are a few I have seen multiple times, but it's not like we are on a first name basis. Anyone who has been with the boss, sure I keep their faces in mind, I'd lose my job if I didn't do that, and hassled the wrong person. But the rest, it's all a sea of stuffed shirts and bras.

It's a quarter 'til four when I feel a tap on my shoulder. "Hey, big fella."

It's the brunette. She has a little color in her face, but she is far from drunk. Her eyes are vibrant, but not glassy. She smiles and tilts her head and man am I falling for her.

"Oh, hi there…" I trail off, no name coming as I never had one. I cough and then smile as she laughs at my embarrassment.

"It's Catherine. But you can call me Cat."

"Okay, Cat. I'm —"

"Darrell. I know, I asked one of the bartenders." She extends her hand and I shake it. "Pleased to meet you, Darrell."

I stand there looking like a dazed idiot, no doubt. I don't mean I've never been approached by a woman, but never by one as fine as this, who as far as I could tell wasn't stoned, wasn't ugly, wasn't anyone that would normally give a guy like me the time of day.

"So, can a girl get a ride home?"

"Sure, sure. No problem, if you can give me fifteen minutes. I got to help close up."

"Okay, Darrell. You can have fifteen minutes, but that's fifteen minutes we won't get to share."

I stick my head in the door, yell at Kenny to come over. He handles security on the inside of the club. We usually lock up and do a once over together. I step into the club as he approaches.

"Kenny, man, can you do me a favor? I got a hot one, man I have to go now or I might lose her. Please, cover for me."

Kenny peeks outside. He lets out a whistle. "Dude, I don't know what lie you told her, but I salute you. For that chick, I will cover for you. Get out of here."

We slap hands and I walk back outside. "Okay, Catherine – I mean Cat. Let's get out of here."

C^{at}

It's a typical Wednesday. Tina, Becky and I meet for coffee downtown after work. They talk me into going clubbing, but I tell them only if we go early and don't close the place down. I do not want another Thursday morning hangover. They agree, so we split up to go get ready. They meet me with a taxi outside my apartment building about nine-thirty.

We heard about a newer place, Rico's, so we head that way. Supposed to be the latest and greatest, and Tina and Becky are on the prowl for fresh meat. Me, I just want to forget about work for a couple hours, do a little dancing, and get home safe.

The line is short and we get to the front pretty quickly. The doorman pretends he's going to stop three women dressed in skin tight dresses and high heels from entering. I smooch up to him. He's pretty nice, a big fella, with a real huggable look to him. Someone normal, not one of the high flying lawyers, fast track yuppies or flashy drug dealers that we'll find inside. He's pretty easy to butter up and before you know it we are inside the club where the music isn't quite full blast yet, the air is only partially hazy from cigarettes and cigars and the place is half empty.

But the half that is populated does not disappoint — not Tina and Becky anyway. A mixture of cultures, races, men and women, with the common denominator being cold hard cash. The place drizzles with it. And every one of them here for something. Power trips, massaging their egos, wanting to be seen. Dealing or being dealt with. Tina and Becky are going to have a field day, I realize, as I see them scoping out the lay of the room. I guess it is not going to be an early night after all, but I swear there will be no hangover. Three drinks max, after that it is water for this girl.

We head over to the bar, walking slow, chatting among ourselves, flashing our pretty smiles. It works. By the time we get there a group of four men has intercepted us and quickly orders our drinks. They are handsome, young, and so shallow I am surprised they are visible in the dim light.

By my fourth drink am sitting at a small corner table with one of them – Larry is his name, I think. It seems like he is different than the others, that he is really listening to me talk about work, about how hard it was to get funding for the Crisis Center.

"Say, who's that your girlfriend is dancing with?" Larry asks.

I turn to look and see Tina dancing with a sharply dressed – well, that was obvious, who wasn't in here? – young black man. I don't recognize him, and am about to tell that to Larry when I see the furtive movement out of the corner of my eye. I shoot my arm back across the table and grab his hand.

"Hey, what gives?"

I dig into his hand with my fingernails, forcing him to open his clenched fist. Two small pills nestle in the palm.

"You son of a…"

"Hey, it's not what you think. You were uptight, had a rough day. I just wanted to help you relax."

"You didn't want me to relax. You wanted to drug me so you could take me home and rape me."

"No, that's not it at all." He looks around, then back at me. He sees I am not buying it. He gets up and runs out of the bar. I want to shout out, to have someone stop him, but the music is so loud now no one would have heard me.

God, what am I doing? I look at the drink on the table. My fourth, I believe. My fourth when I was only going to have three. I get up and walk to the bar. A man standing there tries to order me a drink but I shake my head and tell the bartender I just want a water. I sit down at the bar and slowly sipp the cold glass, looking to the other side of the bar into the large mirror, trying to figure out just who that is staring back at me.

Where did Cat go, I wonder. Where was that smart, independent woman who would never have sat down with a jerk like Larry, let alone almost let him drug her? Somehow she was getting lost. The Crisis Center, that was important work, she knew that. But what about life outside of work? Who was she, that she would end up in a glitzy club like Rico's at three a.m. in the middle of the week?

I look in the mirror again, not at myself but at the people behind me, the now packed club a sea of glamorous people, dancing, drinking, making out with one another in the dark corners. These are not my people, I think. I do not belong here.

Becky comes over. She tells me Tina and her are heading to an after hours place. I shake my head at the invitation to join them. "No thanks, you girls go on. I have to be at work early tomorrow. I'll talk to you later."

She hugs me goodbye and I watch her join Tina and a couple guys. They all look smooth and pretty and like a perfect double date. Good for them, it's what they want. Not for me, though. Not people like that. Like that. Like Tina and Becky, I realize. I have absolutely nothing in common with them. If it wasn't for meeting them at a party a couple years ago when I first moved here, I would never have been friends with them. If you can call drinking coffee twice a week and going to parties where they go one way and I go another being friends.

I wonder if it is just the lateness of the hour, or the aftereffects of the four drinks, or just a bad mood. I guess I'll find out tomorrow —or rather later today. The place is starting to empty now, a sudden shift in the flow of bodies. I glance at my watch and see that another half hour has gone by while I have been musing about my life. My life. It seems like something is missing, something beyond work. Something to help me be strong. Someone to make me feel safe, to feel normal, to feel like it's okay to not even want to belong with this crowd of people in the club.

I think about the only time tonight that I actually felt good. It was the doorman. When I was talking with him, getting us in the place, it felt good. It felt easy and normal, like talking to someone who listened to your words. I ask the bartender who was watching the door. Darrell – that's a solid name. I like that name. I get up, knowing what I want to do now.

A few minutes later and we are walking to a cab. I reach out and take his arm. It feels good. We get into the cab and Darrell gives him an address for a building in a not so nice neighborhood.

We get there and go up to the door of the apartment building. Darrell is fumbling for his keys when I put out my hand and stop him. "Darrell."

He looks at me, a big old teddy bear. "What's the matter?"

I smile. "Nothing. I just – I don't think I can do this."

He crumbles before me. I know I should be a little worried, concerned that this large man is going to take offense at my leading him on, going to hurt me, but I don't get that feeling at all.

He gives a little laugh. "Okay, Cat. I should have known, someone like you, someone like me. I understand."

*** 57 ***

I lean in, put my hands on his shoulders, pull myself up to his face and give him a soft kiss. "It's not that, Darrell. This just isn't the way I want it to start. I think I really like you, I don't want it to be some cheap one night stand."

He stands there, silent, as my words sink in. I hope that I haven't messed this up, haven't misread this guy. Please, I think, please be the nice, safe, normal man I need.

He slowly smiles, hugs me tight and I feel like I could stay in those warm arms forever. I look up into his brown eyes, and there is no hint of Larry, no hint of Rico's, in them.

I get lucky – the cabbie was filling out paperwork and hasn't left. Darrell opens the door for me. I suddenly realize I don't have any cash on me. I turn to him. "I'm sorry, Darrell, but could you lend me the cab fare?"

He reaches into his wallet and hands me a twenty dollar bill. "Now you have to see me again."

I nod. "You can bet on that, big fella."

The cabbie takes me to my building, the change in neighborhood drastic for just a twelve block drive. I hand him the twenty and tell him to keep the change. It's been a good night.

S^{tan}

It's my last call for the night. Usual pickup, couple from one of the late hours clubs. Big guy and a sweet looking girl. I flip the meter on and head to the address the guy gives me.

They sit quietly while I drive, none of the usual after-partying talk, or one of the drunk make out sessions I've seen just as often. It doesn't take long to get to the apartment building, and nothing but my old 70's station on the radio to interrupt the silence of the drive.

The big guy pays me the fare and a couple dollars extra, more than I expected from him, but I guess this little lady has him flying high tonight. I watch them walk up to the entrance and then turn my In Service light off. I radio into Louis that I am done for the night. I start filling in the paperwork for my shift. I'm halfway through when there's a tap on the window. The lady is looking in through the passenger window, waving at me.

I roll the window down. She smiles, a beautiful, gorgeous face bright despite the dim lighting from the buzzing streetlamp. "Can you drive me home?"

Guess the guy isn't flying so high tonight after all. Why not, I think. I keep the meter off. This is on my time; I did my shift. What Louis doesn't know won't hurt him. I unlock the door. "Sure," I tell her, and am rewarded with another smile.

She starts to get in before turning back to the big guy, who stands protectively over her on the sidewalk. I watch her kiss him goodbye after getting a bill from him, then she gets into the back seat and tells me her address.

I pull away from the curb. I look in the mirror. For someone who isn't staying over with the guy she was with, she seems pretty happy. That's something I really don't see that much of, not on the graveyard shift. They usually stay over, or come into the cab upset at either their man or themselves for whatever argument is sending them home. I find myself wondering what's so special about that guy to get a girl like this crazy about him — because it is clear she is, even if she isn't sleeping with him tonight. He seemed like just an average, ordinary Joe to me. Another big lug, more brawn than brains, sure couldn't be his bankroll, not in that neighborhood where I dropped him off.

Curiosity, late night boredom, whatever it is, it gets the better of me. "Why him?" I ask.

She turns from gazing out the window, meets my eyes in the mirror. "Excuse me?"

I want to just forget it but it has a hold of me now. I plow on. "That guy. Why him, instead of some lawyer or politician? A girl like you, you could do better than that guy."

She laughs. "God, to be honest, I don't know." She purses her lips, shakes her head. "I didn't even know him until — well, I still don't really know him. I don't know his full name, or what he likes, what he doesn't like, where he's from. But when I met him he just seemed... right. Like who I was meant to be with. Someone I could trust. Maybe he seems like just another guy to you, maybe he isn't rich or powerful, but those people aren't better than he is. I do know that much."

I could tell the conversation was as strange for her as for me, that she was not used to opening up her inner heart to a cabbie in the middle of the night. I could tell this guy affected her so much, so quickly, so deeply, that she was answering a hack's personal questions without hesitation, straightforward, no bull. I look back to the road, make the next turn. "Man, I wish I had that. I wish I knew that about someone, just by meeting them."

We get to her place and I pull in close to the curb. I take a rough guess at what the fare would be had the meter been on and tell her it's ten bucks. She gives me a twenty and tells me to keep the change. I watch her walk into her building, a much nicer building than the one I left her man in, make sure she gets into it safely. Not that there is much to be concerned about in this area, but at this time of night in the city a pretty girl like that isn't safe on her own anywhere. Except maybe with a man like she found. To have someone like her think about me the way she does for that guy. He didn't have anything on me, he was just another guy. Nothing on me but someone like her.

I want to go home, but a desire to feel as good as they did was stronger than the need for sleep. Well, there's no lady around, not for me, but there are other ways to feel good. I drive back toward the neighborhood we had left her man in.

I pull into a Quickie Mart with poor lighting in the parking lot. Wouldn't take long, I knew, even though this particular spot was new to me. I am right: fifteen minutes later a young man in a hoodie walks by. My window is already rolled down and I let out a "pssst" to get his attention.

He strolls over, giving darting glances around the lot to make sure he is aware of who's in the area, who might be watching. "What's up?"

I keep my voice low. "Looking for something to relax me, man. Can you help me out?"

He looks around again before leaning down, resting his elbows on the driver side door. "Maybe. What'cha got?"

I show him the twenty. "Just need something for tonight, nothing heavy. A little something to smoke."

He reaches into the front pocket of his hoodie, pulls out a medium-sized joint. "Sure man, I can help you, this here will treat you right."

I flash three fingers. "How about a couple more to go with that one?"

He laughs. "No, man, can't give you three for that, Gee would kill me." He puts the first joint back in the pocket, pulls out two smaller ones. "I can do this for twenty."

I nod, hand over the twenty and take the two tightly-rolled cigarettes. "Thanks, man." I roll up the window, put the cab in drive and head home to find my own good feeling.

Jay-23

Nothing much going on. Sold most of my stuff inside Dirty Ben's, a club down on Madison. Have a few joints and a little bit of ecstasy left. Figure I am done for the night so I start walking home.

I'm cutting through the parking lot of the Quickie Mart when this white dude in a taxi cab calls me over. I look around. Nobody else in the lot, a couple cars parked on the street but no one in them. I walk over to see what he wants.

He's buying. Should have known, no other reason for a cab to be parked here at this time of the night. I don't recognize him but I can smell a cop a mile away and he's no cop. He tries to bargain with me. I gotta account for every pill, every joint – no way am I going to cut deals, especially with a stranger. I offer him two small ones for his twenty, he falls for it. Sucker doesn't know the street price, that I would have taken fifteen for them, or that the one he turned down was worth more than the two little ones combined.

Not bad to add a little extra to the night's take. I got over three grand; for a Wednesday night that's better than average. Gee will let me keep a hundred and fifty of it. I'll get three times that on a Friday or Saturday.

I head on home. Only run into a couple other people, nobody with any money. The locals know me, know to leave me alone. You don't mess with one of Gee's boys, not in this neighborhood. Not if you want to see tomorrow.

It's past five by the time I unlock the deadbolt and enter our apartment. Mom is passed out on the couch. I walk across the living room and find my little brother in the kitchen.

"What's up, David?"

He turns away from the stove, smiles at me. "Hey, Jay. I'm just trying to make oatmeal for Whitney."

I point a finger at him. "I told you, David, call me Jay-23."

"Whatever." He turns back to the stove, stirs the pot.

I walk closer and lean over him, looking into the boiling mixture. "Man, it's too thick. You gotta add more milk. It'll thicken up after you cook it, when it sits for awhile."

"We're out of milk."

I glance back across kitchen counter to the living room, shaking my head at Mom. "She didn't go to work last night, did she?"

David shuffles his feet, pretends he is concentrating on the oatmeal.

I grab his arm, harder than I intended to, and he winces as I ask him, "Did she?"

"No. She was going to, and then…"

I don't release my grip. I know I am hurting him but I wait for him to finish.

"She took the money."

I tighten my grip and almost shout at him, "She took the grocery money? Again?"

He nods. "She can't help it, Jay. She wants to be good. She just can't help it."

He's sniffling, trying to hold in the tears. Whitney must have heard me yelling because I can hear her in the bedroom, crying for Mom. I shake my head, release David and bite my lip as he rubs his arm where I had grabbed him. I am not shouting anymore. "I know, David. I know she tries." I reach into my pocket and pull out a twenty dollar bill. "Here, take this. Get something good for lunch at school. Go ahead, I'll feed Whitney."

He wipes his nose with his sleeve. "Thanks, Jay."

I point my finger at him, give him a stern look.

He smiles, tears drying, points a finger back at me. "Jay-23."

D avid

I get up early. Mom's on the couch. I guess I have to feed Whitney again. Don't know where Jay is. I hardly ever see him anymore. It's not like it used to be, when he would take me to the park and shoot hoops. Now he's always running around with his friends. People he doesn't even want me to meet. I'm not stupid. I know what's going on with him and his so-called friends. I'm twelve, not six.

I look in the fridge. Nothing but old ketchup and moldy cheese. I should have known when I saw Mom on the couch, the empty bottle lying on its side on the coffee table, that she hadn't bought any groceries. My stomach rumbled at the thought of another day at school without lunch.

I have to find something for Whitney to eat. I open up the corner cupboard, search behind the half-melted plastic bowls and find the oatmeal. I look on the back of the box. Supposed to add milk. I pour some into a pot and add water instead. I pour an extra cup of oatmeal in to make up for the missing milk, hoping that will make it nutritious enough for Whitney. Don't have anything else to make, I guess it will have to do.

Once I feed Whitney I can walk her over to Alice's. Don't want to leave her with Mom. Have to leave by six so I can make it to school on time. Today's my favorite day, we get to go downtown to the main library. I remember the permission slip and the lunch money for eating out stashed in my backpack. I think about Mom and the bottle. I leave the pot simmering and rush to the door where my backpack leans against the wall.

It's gone. She took my money, the money Jay gave me so I could go to the library and eat at McDonald's with the rest of my class. I want to yell, to run over to the couch and wake her up and ask her why she hates me, why she has to ruin everything for me. I crumple up the permission slip, holding onto it tightly in a curled up ball in my fist, until my fingernails bite into my skin and draw blood.

I open my fist and smooth the paper, place it back into my backpack. Doesn't matter. I'll just get my books and find a corner to read, the heck with McDonald's.

I go back to the kitchen and stir the oatmeal. It doesn't look right, it is too lumpy and I wonder how I will get Whitney to eat it. I hear the deadbolt slide in the door and Jay comes in. He looks tired, like he's been walking all night.

Jay figures out what Mom did. He also tells me what's wrong with the oatmeal, gives me twenty bucks so I can go to McDonald's and then says he will take care of Whitney this morning. I love Jay, I do. And times like this, I can tell he still loves me, too.

I grab my backpack and put the money in with the permission slip, then take off for school. I'm happy, thinking about McDonald's and finding books at the library and shooting hoops with Jay. Not thinking about Mom. Nope, today is a good day, and those thoughts don't fit it.

I get to school early, since I didn't have to take Whitney to Alice's. I see Jefferson, my best friend, hanging out in the school yard. I tell him about Jay giving me money, tell him I have enough so he can eat there too. Jefferson's mom doesn't give him money either, but he usually has bologna sandwiches. But who wants to eat bologna sandwiches when the rest of your class is eating at McDonald's?

We start talking about Big Macs and Super Size French fries and all the free refills of Coke we can drink. We talk too loudly, I guess, because Tyrone Banks comes over and next thing I know two of his gang are holding me while he goes through my backpack. He laughs and holds up the twenty dollar bill.

"Don't you know who his big brother is?" Jefferson shouts at them. "He's Jay-23. He runs with Gee. You guys better give that back if you know what's good for you."

Everyone freezes. The two boys holding me let go, their arms falling to their sides and they step back from me. Tyrone looks at Jefferson, looks back at me. He sees the rest of the kids watching us. He holds the bill, looking like he wants to drop it and run but knowing what that would look like if he did.

"Jay-23 is your brother?"

I look at him, meet his stare. My brother, the drug dealer. The gang member. From what I've heard, the murderer. My brother? My Jay, who played hoops with me and makes sure Whitney gets to Alice's safely and gives me money for lunch so I can eat at McDonald's with everyone else? Jay is my brother, not Jay-23.

I know I could admit it and he would believe me, would give me the twenty back and leave Jefferson and me alone for the rest of the school year. I could tell him that, but it would take more from me than twenty bucks to believe Jay-23 is my real brother.

"No," I tell him. "I don't know any Jay-23."

Tyrone pushes Jefferson hard, knocking him to the ground. He flaps the twenty in the air, then shoves it into his pocket. "Nice try, punk." He and his gang walk off.

Jefferson looks up at me. I reach to help him up but he avoids my hand, pushes himself up off the ground. "Why'd you lie, David? Why'd you let him take the money?

All you had to do was tell him yes, to let him know who your brother was."

Jefferson's my best friend. I want to explain it to him, but I can't. To him, I have just thrown away the most street cred anyone in the sixth grade could have. I had given away safety, respect, protection – I had thrown away McDonald's.

T yrone

Dad is driving me to school. It's his way of trying to keep in touch with his kid. As if twenty minutes of listening to him talking into his cell phone while avoiding other cars, occasionally honking at them and giving them the finger when they fail to yield, is going to bond us together. He pauses his conversation long enough to unlock the door when we pull up to the unloading zone at school. "See you tonight."

Whatever. I push the door open, get out and slam it as hard as I can behind me. I can hear him yell through the glass. He's back on the phone as he pulls out in front of a mini-van and speeds away.

I walk over to the front steps. Jason and Brandon are already there. "What's up, boys?"

Brandon shrugs. "Nothing much. Another stupid school day."

"At least we get out for a while today," Jason says.

I look at him questioningly.

"Field trip, man. Sure, it's the city library, but that's better than classes."

Oh, crap. I look back at the unloading zone, but of course Dad hasn't pulled around the block and returned with my book bag. Why would he notice that sitting on the passenger side when he doesn't even notice when I am there? Not that he would have interrupted his work schedule to turn around and bring me my book bag with the permission slip inside my math book even if he had noticed it.

I turn back to Jason. "Who wants to go to the library? It's just a bunch of stupid books."

"Hey, they got a cool graphic novel section now. I heard there's some stuff you can't buy without an ID."

This blows. Only field trip that I could have found something that interested me and I can't go.

"Besides," Brandon adds, "it beats sitting in study hall with Dennison."

Jason nods. "Yeah, I don't want to be stuck with him for three hours."

"I guess," I tell them. I start walking around the school. I don't want to go to study hall with that old fossil, but it was too late to try to find a blank permission slip and forge Dad's signature. This was going to suck.

We find a couple runts joking around on the side lot. They're talking about going to the library and eating at McDonald's, something else I won't be doing today. Why should this little punk get to go on a field trip? Why does his dad care enough to make sure he has his permission slip, and money for lunch, too?

Screw that. I get Brandon and Jason to hold him while I search his backpack. I fish the money out. Holy crap, twenty bucks, this kid must be rich. Too bad for him, too good for me.

The kid's friend tries to tell me the kid is connected. Jay-23, that's serious. I look at the kid, a scared little punk. Sure doesn't look like his brother runs with Gee, but you can never tell for sure, and I sure don't want to mess with that crowd. The kid folds and admits he isn't Jay-23's brother. I shove his friend to the ground for trying to fool me and walk away, putting the twenty dollar bill away in my front pocket.

"I'm ditching," I tell Brandon and Jason.

"What?" Brandon asks.

"You heard me. I ain't going to the library. I'm cutting out as soon as they let us out to go to the bus. You guys with me?"

They look at each other. I knew it. They don't have the guts. I save them the trouble of making up an excuse. "Ah, forget it. I was just kidding. I'm going to study hall. I'd rather sit there and get under Dennison's skin than go to the library and mess around with a bunch of lame books."

The first bell rings and we head into the school building. At ten-thirty Mrs. Winslow leads us out to the bus. I hang back as the other kids hand her their permission slips. I tell her I don't have one and she sighs heavily, as if my not going to the library was going to cause the end of the world, and then sends me off to Dennison's room.

I take a left at the end of the hall and hide in the bathroom for fifteen minutes, until I am sure the bus has left. I sneak out of the school and start walking.

Not a whole lot to do on a Thursday when all your friends are in school. I start heading towards home, figuring something will come up between here and there. If nothing else I'll put in a DVD until just before Dad gets home. Throw my school books on the kitchen table, add a couple pieces of paper with scribbled writing on them, he'll never know I skipped.

About halfway home I decide spending the rest of a school day watching TV would be a waste. I can do that any day. Got to be something else to do, something I can't do at home. I stick my hands in my pocket, feel the twenty dollar bill there. I think about the library and the graphic novel section. Suddenly I know what to do.

I cut across Norton Street to get to Eddie's Comic World. Eddie's a loser, but he has the best comic shop in town. All the new stuff, and boxes and boxes of back issues. Of course, you have to listen to him whenever you buy something. That always blows, but with twenty bucks I could get something good — something worth listening to Eddie, even.

Fifteen minutes later I push open the door to Comic World. Eddie sits where he always is when no one is in the shop, on the couch in the middle of the store staring up at the TV he has hanging from the ceiling, watching some anime movie.

"Tyrone."

His squeaky voice makes me want to leave, but I really have nothing better to do, and I want to get what I came for.

"Eddie. What's up?"

He gestures at the TV. "It's Thursday, day after Wednesday. What do you think?"

New books come in on Wednesdays, almost everyone buys them Wednesday night. Plus it's still school hours, so the place is empty except for Eddie and me. I shrug. I wasn't really asking, didn't really care what this loser did, only cared what he could give me.

I stand there for a while, watching Eddie watch the movie. After a few minutes he blinks, turns to me as if he didn't realize I was still there, and asks, "Did you want something?"

I nod.

"Oh, well, the new *Mutanika Squadron* came in yesterday."

I shake my head. "I don't want that crap. I want something good."

Eddie reaches for the remote, pauses the movie. He turns to me, eyes narrow, nose twitching like some money radar just went off in his head. "Really? How good?"

I pull out the twenty and hold it out with both hands so he can easily see the bill. "This good." I pause, let the sweat bead on his forehead. "Issue seventeen of *The Atomic Squid* good."

"Oh my God." Eddie gets up, his pasty face turning red. He starts wheezing and for a moment I think the guy's going to have a heart attack. I look around and wonder what all I could grab before the ambulance would get here.

Eddie takes a deep breath and then starts in with his voice squeaking higher than before. "Issue seventeen," he manages to get out, as he leans against the back of the sofa, "where the Atomic Squid learns that the mastermind behind the death of his beloved Brenda Barracuda is none other than Clive, his own sixth tentacle?"

I keep cool, trying to hide the fact that I am as excited about the best comic ever created as Eddie is. "Yeah, that one."

Eddie squints, looks at the twenty dollar bill and then back at me. "You serious?"

"I got twenty bucks, you got the comic," I tell him, pointing at the very issue displayed on the rack behind the counter.

Eddie walks behind the counter. He stares at the cover, the Atomic Squid logo in blazing red against the blue sea background, the bold declaration that this issue reveals all, the corpse of Brenda Barracuda nestled in his tentacles. I swear, Eddie looks like he is going to cry.

He takes it off the shelf and carefully places it on the counter. I reach out for it and Eddie puts out a hand to stop me.

"Uh-uh," he says. "No touching until you buy it. This baby is in mint condition, I don't want any grimy fingerprints on it."

"How do I know it's mint unless I look at it?"

Eddie wheezes. "You been buying comics here for three, four years, Tyrone. You think I don't know mint condition? Have I ever mis-graded a book?"

I know he hasn't. This guy is too much of a geek to ever call something mint that wasn't. I slide the twenty across the counter. "Fine. Now give it to me."

He looks like he wants to change his mind, that he doesn't want to let it go, but finally he places the comic in my hands. I look at the dynamic cover through the clear plastic bag. Issue seventeen. I can't believe it, I finally got issue seventeen.

I head over to the door, clutching the comic firmly.

Eddie calls out before I get through the door, "Don't forget to change the bag and board once a year!"

I look back at his pasty face. He looks like he just sold his best friend. "Yeah, sure. I just want to read it."

E ddie

I'm watching *Akitachi Assassin*. I read online that there is a frame where Akitachi only has three fingers. So far twelve viewings have not revealed the frame with the error.

The door opens and one of the punk kids that comes in once a week to buy the latest mutant drivel comes in. Tyrone, that's his name. In this business, you have to remember their names, what they like, what they can't stand – God help you if you push a DC comic to a Marvel fan – basically have to treat them like their favorite comic is the second coming of *Watchmen*. Not that any of these kids even know what that is. It's all crap. Nobody cares about the story anymore, it's all flashy art with as much skin showing as possible. Bunch of hacks writing them, half the time the story doesn't even make sense but these kids don't even notice. Most of them probably can't even read. Nobody cares about continuity, about plot and structure. It's like watching a freaking Star Trek episode – just use the stupid device you invented two shows ago, you morons.

After about five minutes of ignoring him the kid is still there. His mom probably dropped him off while she went shopping. Parents think I'm a free babysitter, that they can just drop their kids off here for an hour or so, not considering that once they wrinkle up a comic or get their sticky fingers on the cover no one will buy it and I will have to stick it in the quarter box at a loss.

When Tyrone says he doesn't want yesterday's *Mutanika Squadron*, that he wants a real comic, something good, I pause the movie. The three-fingered assassin can wait. I smell money on the kid.

I take back my earlier comments; this kid is not the usual punk, despite most of the crap he has bought from me in the past. He asks for issue seventeen of *The Atomic Squid.* The penultimate storyline in modern comics, the Macbeth of the current age. Somehow, under the punk exterior, this kid has discovered what comics are really about, what true magnificence can be achieved by the right blend of art and words.

I go behind the counter and take the comic from its place on the rack, holding it at the edges to avoid any potential creases. The cover shines under the clear protective plastic mylar bag, held firmly in place with the acid-free white backing board underneath the comic. All four corners perfectly cut, colors clear and sharp, logo and front image centered, spine nice and tight, staples firm. A true gem. A pristine copy in mint condition. Price guides undervalue this issue, not recognizing the genius of the storyline culminating in this issue, feeling the art is not flashy enough, not cutting edge. No gimmicky hologram on the cover, just the dynamic logo, the poignant pose of the Squid carrying his fallen love, and the tantalizing promise in bold lettering that all would be revealed inside.

I eye the twenty that Tyrone is holding out, block his first attempt to grab the comic from the counter. I see it, though, in his eyes. I see that he does know how good this comic is, that it represents the best the industry has to offer. For ten bucks he could get this same issue at Howling Wolf Comics on the other side of the city, but it would not be in this condition. And for this comic, that matters. The best comic in the best condition. I have no qualms about charging him twenty for this. It is truly priceless.

I put the twenty into my pocket. It came from my personal collection and will not be listed on the day's receipts. I gasp when I see Tyrone hold onto the book too tightly. Surely such a grip has caused a minor crease along the spine. No mint book can remain in true mint condition with that kind of rough handling. I yell at him as he leaves, reminding him to change the bag and board annually to protect it. He shrugs it off.

I feel hollow inside. The comic is lost, already down to near mint condition by the time the door closed. It will have folded corners, rolled over spine, nasty creases by the second reading. Stupid punks. No sense of history.

I sit back down on the couch to look for the three-fingered assassin. I will go frame by frame, again, until I find it.

Three hours later I freeze the DVD. Is that it? I stand up, look closely at the monitor. Yes! No pinkie, an artist error. I decide to order pizza to celebrate the victory.

I call up Montoni's. I order the works. It is well past my usual lunch time, and I am starving. Hard work, holding up the standard for artistic perfection. I sit back down on the couch to wait for the pizza to be delivered.

J eanie

Montoni's started opening up earlier for lunch a month ago. Who the heck orders pizza at ten-thirty in the morning, I asked Chris, but he waved me off and said not everyone eats lunch at noon. Guess he knew what he was talking about because we've been just as busy between ten and noon as we are between two and four in the afternoon. We're still busiest right around noon, and then after five, but it has been steady enough to justify the extra hours. And morning tippers generally give me an extra buck or two, and that sure helps.

I'm glad we're busy. I would rather have the day go by fast, with one delivery after another, than sit on my butt with nothing to do. Better busy than bored, that's what I always say.

I volunteered to cover the extra hours if Chris would give me every other Friday night off. I hated to give up the Friday deliveries, it's good steady business, but I wanted to get a three day weekend twice a month so I could visit Wayne. Wayne's my brother. He's upstate, serving twenty years for armed robbery. He did it, he admitted it, but all he had was a pocket knife. That judge, he just didn't like Wayne's long hair. He didn't even listen when Wayne said he was sorry, when even the car owner said he forgave him. He just said twenty years and banged the gavel down and they took my brother off in handcuffs.

But what's done is done, that's what I always say, and if that means I go visit Wayne once a month and try to make his world a little brighter then that is what I will do. And when Chris came up with the morning hours, and then let me work those and take every other Friday off, well that was the Good Lord finding a way for me to visit Wayne more often. It was like God made people hungry for pizza at ten in the morning so I could help my brother keep on the straight and narrow while he is locked up with all those criminals.

Tomorrow I will take off right after the lunch rush and head upstate to the Cranston State Prison. I have been clipping newspaper articles and saving magazines for Wayne, lots of ideas on how he can make his days more productive. So he can come out in fourteen years – ten if he continues on his good behavior – and make something good with his life. Different ways to serve the Lord, to make the world a better place. I tell him that is why God has him confined, so that he can concentrate, so he can take advantage of the days of solitude to meditate on His wonders. Wayne doesn't always see it that way, though. He always asks me why the Good Lord allowed him to get so drunk he was stupid enough to try to steal a police car using his fishing knife. What can you say to that but that the Lord works in mysterious ways?

Anyway it has been a good morning and now we are in the middle of the noon rush. I enjoy delivering pizzas, always with a smile and a God Bless You. If they look like they aren't exactly the praying type I say a quick Our Father for them when I get back to my car. There are a lot of our customers that don't seem like the praying type. But sometimes they surprise you. Just a couple weeks ago there was this big guy in a sleeveless t-shirt with tattoos up one arm and down the other and three earrings in each ear, large hoops that looked like they could go around my wrist. Well, when I gave him the pizza box and he handed me the money and gave me a two dollar tip, I smiled and said "God bless you" and he gave me the biggest smile in return and told me "Amen, sister, amen." That just made my day!

I go to the counter. Chris has five boxes stacked on top of each other. I check the addresses. He sometimes forgets to put them in order. I rearrange the stack so my first delivery is on top and the two boxes for the last delivery on the bottom, then slide the stack into my insulated warmer. It does a good job of keeping the pizzas hot, as long as I don't get stuck at too many red lights.

The first delivery is a regular customer. One glance and I know the exact route I will take to get me to Eddie's Comic Shop the quickest. He must have had a good day, he ordered the works instead of the usual one-topping special for $9.95.

My drive goes smoothly and I open up the door to the comic shop with one hand while balancing the insulated warmer on my other arm. "Good afternoon, Eddie," I tell him, giving him my best regular-customer smile.

"Hey Jeanie."

He gets up off the couch. Inside I am shaking my head. He seems like a good man, but he spends all his time watching cartoons and selling trashy comics to kids. He should get a good job, should spend his time with the Bible and helping kids out. Well, judge not lest ye be judged, I always say, so I continue to smile as I take his order from the warmer.

"$14.95," I say, laying the box on the counter.

Eddie digs into his pocket and pulls out a twenty dollar bill. He hands it to me. "Just give me a couple bucks back, Jeanie."

I unzip my pocket and take out my money envelope. I place the twenty inside and take out two singles and hand them back to Eddie. "Thank you, Eddie. God bless you."

He half smiles and nods. Eddie is one of the ones who needs a good praying for. He takes the box over to the couch. He has a slice out and the cartoon started again before the door closes behind me.

I say a quick Our Father for Eddie after I get to the car. I make two more deliveries before my last one for this trip. I recheck the final address and start heading to Lutheran Drive. This is a nice area, at the very edge of our delivery zone. Single family homes instead of strip malls and apartment buildings. The people here, they need a lot of prayers. The Good Lord has blessed them with earthly riches, and those are the people who find it hardest to part with material things, to let the Good Lord work his miracles in their lives.

I ring the doorbell. A pretty young girl, couldn't be more than six or seven, answers. She sees the pizza and runs away, leaving the door wide open. "Pizza's here! Pizza's here!" she shouts as she runs into the house.

I wait outside the door. Soon enough her mother, I presume, comes to the door. She looks tired. I give her my best new-customer smile and say, "One pepperoni and mushroom pizza, $12.95."

She doesn't smile back. "One minute, please, let me get my purse." She walks down the hall and picks up a black leather purse. She fumbles through it. She comes back to me holding a single crisp bill. "All I have is a fifty, is that okay?"

I don't point to my button that reads "Drivers carry less than $20 in change." But she sees it anyway. She purses her lips, frowns, deep wrinkles showing up on her forehead and at the corners of her mouth. "Let me see if I have something smaller."

"It's okay," I tell her. "This is my last stop on this delivery run, I can make change for you." It's not something I would tell many of my customers. Do not lead others into temptation, that's what I always say, but I do not think that this woman will be tempted by my having more than twenty dollars in change. I unzip my pocket and take out my envelope. I accept the fifty dollar bill from her and hand her a twenty, a ten, a five, two ones and a nickel. She gives me a single dollar back. I smile and say "God bless you."

The little girl starts screaming for pizza in the other room and the mother takes the pizza from me. I go out to the car and say an Our Father for her and a Hail Mary for the little girl.

C harlotte

Ben left on another road trip this morning. Left me with the kids, again. And after Rosita quit yesterday. I had to do the laundry last night, was up early this morning to iron Ben's dress shirts. Why that man can't learn to iron his own shirts… Katie and Ben Junior were up early of course, just when I wanted to lay back down for a nap. Katie wanted waffles and Ben Junior wanted pancakes and they both sulked when I gave them cold cereal instead. What do people expect? I've been busy with fundraisers and working on my book, how am I going to find time to cook and clean too? I still can't believe Rosita left. It's like she couldn't get out of here fast enough, after three years of working here and then she gives no notice whatsoever and she's gone.

I finally get the kids to eat their cereal by promising they can have pizza for lunch. After putting the breakfast dishes in the dishwasher I set them in front of the TV and go into my office and try to write. It is a slow, laborious morning, and by noon I don't even have five hundred decent words to show for my efforts. I just can't get into it today, I'm all worn out and beat up. How can you create exciting characters and dialogue when your conversations consist of arguing with five and seven year old children about who got the biggest piece of pie or why their socks are on the floor and not in the hamper?

But somehow, someway, I am going to get this darn thing out of me. I've been trying to write a modern *Gone With The Wind* for five years now. I know the lead character, I feel her in my bones, struggling to get out and express her independence, her fiery spirit, her passion and love and hate. It's her counterpart I can't seem to get out. The male lead, her inspiration, her opposition, her partner – he has to be all that for it to work. But somehow I can't get to him. Not that surprising, I guess. How can I write about someone like that when all I have to draw on is Ben? Nice, safe, conservative Ben. Not exactly the rip the shirt open and take the breath away type.

I shouldn't complain. There's nothing wrong with Ben. Nothing about him that I really want to change. Maybe he isn't movie star handsome, or rippling with muscles or romantic enough to surprise me with morning kisses or walk in on me in the shower and rekindle the passion that led to our children. But he trudges out week after week on his sales route, he keeps us in this beautiful home in a safe neighborhood, he puts money away every check for the kids' college funds. And he loves me. I know he does, by the small things. How he always remembers to call me before he goes to bed, no matter where he is. How he remembers my favorite songs and turns them up when we are in the car together. How he smiles and brushes his lips across my cheek when he is leaving for another trip.

But those things do not a powerful, magnetic, charismatic hero make. How could a strong woman like my Tessa find her counterpart in Ben? No, I need something more for my book. I need someone vibrant, someone alive, someone larger than life who will challenge, not conquer, my Tessa. Someone like Richard, I am forced to admit.

Richard is Ben's partner. He handles the clients after Ben gets the initial contract in place. Richard is smooth, handsome, and ever since last Christmas when he made a pass at me in our kitchen I have been thinking what it would be like to be with him. Not forever, not anything like that, but just to escape for a night in his arms. When I think of Tessa, what she would want, I think of Richard. And I can't write that, I can't write what their passion would be like, how they would talk to each other, how they would make love to each other, until I know what that is like myself. But how could I do that to Ben? How could I cross that line, just to be able to write my book? I know I can't. Ben doesn't deserve those thoughts.

I work on plotting and outlining since the dialogue and the love scenes are not forthcoming. I keep at it until I hear Katie yelling that the pizza is here. I go to the door. An older woman is delivering it. I wonder what it would be like to be delivering pizza at her age. Where did her life turn so that she was doing this, at her age, instead of in a house taking care of her children – or grandchildren?

I fumble through my purse and can't find anything smaller than a fifty. She gives me the change. I hear the kids yelling and I distractedly give her a tip. It isn't until after she leaves that I realize I gave her a one dollar bill instead of the five I intended to. I want to open up the door and run down the driveway to catch her and give her the five, but then Katie and Ben Junior start screaming for the pizza and instead I go into the kitchen with the box.

I open the box and swear when I see they didn't make it half pepperoni and half mushroom but instead put both ingredients on each side. I take back my regrets at the small tip as I pick off mushrooms from one half and pepperoni from the other half. Katie and Ben Junior carefully inspect the pieces that I place on plates before them, making sure none of the foreign topping has remained on their slices. God only knows what would happen should Katie accidentally eat a pepperoni, or if Ben Junior found a mushroom still on his piece. I put the removed ingredients on top of my own piece and hungrily eat it.

The doorbell rings and I tell the kids to stay and finish eating lunch while I get the door. I open it up. Rosita is standing there, looking meek, wringing her hands, with downcast eyes.

"Hello, Rosita."

"Hello, Mrs. Johnson." She wrings her hands more, making me want to reach out and grab them. "I'm sorry, I just…"

I give in and take her hands in my own. "Rosita. Please, you worked for us for three years. You know me, you know I'm your friend. What do you need?"

She looks up and blinks away tears. "It's just my last pay. I need it for my bus ticket. I left before I could get it yesterday. I didn't know how to ask for it."

"Come on in, I'll get it."

She rubs her hand across her eyes, brushing away her long black hair and the tears at the same time. "No, that's okay, I'll just wait here."

I pause. Something is wrong, clearly, with this poor woman. But to be honest, though I call her friend, what do I really know about her? She has worked for us for three years, but I couldn't tell you where she came from, when her birthday is or why she left yesterday. "How much do we owe you?"

"One hundred, if you could. I did not charge for yesterday."

I get my purse and pull out a hundred dollar bill. I look for the change from the pizza delivery woman and grab it also. I go to the door, press it in Rosita's hands. "Here, take this. You deserve it. I'm sorry it didn't work out for you, here. Ben and I, we both liked you very much. We both wish you well."

"Thank you, Mrs. Johnson. You are very kind. You have been wonderful to me. I just wish…"

I notice she thanks me only, that Ben receives none of her praise. I see her red eyes, brimming with tears. "Rosita, did something happen?"

She shakes her head. "I am sorry, Mrs. Johnson. I have to go, I really do."

She runs down the driveway to a car that is idling. She gets into the passenger door and the car speeds off.

I stand there for a few minutes, the door wide open, wondering about her words, about her sudden departure. I wonder about Ben, and how quiet he was this morning before he left. And then I start wondering about Richard. About what I need in order to write my book.

R osita

It was difficult, yesterday afternoon, telling Mrs. Johnson that I must leave immediately. How could I tell her the truth? I enjoyed my work at their home, cooking with new appliances and cleaning with the best supplies. Their children were relatively well-behaved and did not bother me with my work.

The money was fair, enough to keep my own family both housed and fed, with a little bit left over that I would send home to Momma in her colonia outside of Matamoras each month. Not a lot, but enough to let her stay where she wants to, in the house she grew up in. I wish she would join us but she will not leave, and I cannot find a job in Mexico that will pay enough to take care of my family and Momma as well.

Now, now I do not know what will happen. My cousin Maria is in Atlanta and tells me she has a job lined up for me. So if I can get my final pay from the Johnson's then I will be able to get bus tickets for me, Julio and Margarita. One hundred dollars, that is what the man at the bus station told me it would cost. I do not want to go back there. I do not want to see Mrs. Johnson, to go into that house. It was not right, it should not have happened. I fight to keep the tears in when I think about how it all went wrong.

Mr. Johnson, there have been times in the past when he squeezed by me in the hallway too close, leaning in against me. But that is all it ever was, and most of the time when I worked he was not home, either away on one of his trips or working in his office. Once I had supper started Mrs. Johnson took over, and I would be gone most days before he was home for the night. I could ignore the lustful stares, the occasional brushes in the hallway. We seldom were alone together, and then only for moments before Mrs. Johnson or one of the children came into the room. I never felt endangered.

Yesterday, though, it all changed. Mrs. Johnson had taken the kids to school. She had a meeting with one of her organizations and told me she would not be back until the afternoon. I decided to take advantage of the empty house to do some of the cleaning I had not had a chance to get to earlier in the week. I stripped all the beds down and started a load of sheets in the washer. I got out the mop and bucket and began mopping the hardwood floors. It was hard work, and I was sweating before I was too far into the job.

I did not hear the downstairs door open. I let out a little shriek of surprise when the shadow from the bedroom door fell across the floor. I looked up and Mr. Johnson was there. The look of lust was evident in his stare.

"Rosita."

His voice was low, deep. I held on to the handle of the mop, positioning it between us. "Mr. Johnson, I thought you were at the office."

"I forgot some papers." He looked around the bedroom, glanced at the stripped bed, then back to me. He stepped in closer.

He placed his hands over mine on the mop handle. "Rosita, have I ever told you how beautiful you are?"

I struggled to pull my hands out from under his. He latched onto them, held them tightly and pushed me back and onto the bed, falling down on top of me.

"No!" I screamed. "No!" I pushed against his chest and managed to roll away from him. My blouse was torn, the top button ripped off. I held the fabric together with one hand. "Mr. Johnson, please, do not do this," I pleaded.

He backed away, seeming to gain control of himself again. "Rosita, I'm sorry. I didn't mean anything by it. Please, please don't tell Charlotte."

I was trembling, scared of what he tried to do, what he could still do. I did not meet his eyes, I was afraid of what I might see there. "I won't say anything," I tell him. I would tell him anything to get him to leave, to get him to go away.

He went into the bathroom and I heard him splashing water on his face. I ran downstairs, went to the hall bathroom and locked the door. I heard him standing outside of it a few minutes later. He knocked softly but I ignored it. I jumped when the door knob rattled, but he did not force it open. In a little while I heard the front door slam. I waited for half an hour before I slowly came out. I looked in the driveway for his car and then cautiously checked to make sure every room in the house is empty before feeling safe.

I finished the bedrooms. I had to; I cannot leave the job undone. When Mrs. Johnson comes home I tell her I must leave, that I cannot work there anymore. I run out before she can press me for any more information.

But now I must go back. I need the hundred dollars for the bus fare to Atlanta. I wish I had the money, but there is nothing extra, not since Julio got sick last week and I had to spend the rest of my savings on the medicine. I get my neighbor Francesca to drive me to the Johnson's house. I am relieved that only the mini-van is in the driveway.

I go up and ring the doorbell. Mrs. Johnson answers. It is hard, not to tell her why I have left their house. It is hard not to tell her that Mr. Johnson tried to make love to me. It is hard to take the money from her, but I must.

I rush down the driveway after she has given me the money I asked for. I saw the question in her eyes, saw that she suspected what may have occurred. That is enough, I tell myself. She will figure it out, she will realize the truth about her husband soon.

I tell Francesca to leave and she speeds off. I open my hand and see that Mrs. Johnson has given me extra money, more than I asked for. I try to keep from crying but the tears spill out anyway. Francesca keeps asking what is wrong and I tell her nothing, nothing is wrong, I will be able to send Momma money this week after all.

Francesca takes me home and she waits while I gather the children and our meager possessions. I put the hundred and fifteen dollars in my purse, enough for the bus trip and one meal on the way. I take the twenty dollar bill that Mrs. Johnson included and place it between three folded sheets of paper and put it all in an envelope and address it to Momma. Hopefully the thick paper will hide the cash from her postman, and her neighbors.

Francesca watches the children while I go into the post office and mail the letter to Momma. Then she takes us to the bus station. I kiss and hug her goodbye and thank her for all her help. After we load the suitcases onto the bus I lead Julio and Margarita to our seats. It will be a long ride to Atlanta.

A nna-Maria

I say my morning Rosary. My knees hurt from kneeling so long on the wooden kneelers. My cousin Juanita told me once that the churches in the big cities have soft padding atop the kneelers. It is strange to think of making prayer easier, of giving comfort to our bodies when it is about prostrating ourselves before God. It is God who gives comfort to our souls, we should not be concerned with the softness of where we kneel.

It is not my affair. I say a quick prayer for forgiveness for letting my mind wander while still in the church. I glance at the alms box, thinking about the twenty dollar bill that arrived yesterday, carefully hidden within three sheets of paper covered with my daughter Rosita's beautiful handwriting. No, I will know what it is for, I do not hear God calling for the money yet. I dip my fingers into the font as I leave, letting the holy water soak in where I tap my forehead, stomach and either side of my chest. The wind is still as I walk along the dirt streets. Good, the dust will not be in my eyes today.

I hear a slow rumble behind me and I turn and see the Americans are early today. There are two vans full of them, another mission trip that is building new houses in the colonia. The vans they drive are worth more than all the houses they will build this week combined. But it is still good that they are helping. Good to see houses built with new lumber, with tin roofs that are not rusted out so they actually keep out the rain. Good to see the hope in the eyes of the families when they receive the key to their new twelve by twenty-four foot home that has more than tripled their living space.

My daughter writes to me from the United States, telling me of the enormous houses they have there. You could fit a dozen of our houses in just one floor of their castles, she tells me. She wants me to come and stay with her, Julio and Margarita. I wish I could, I miss them all so much. But this is my home, this is where I grew up. My heart is here; I cannot leave.

My only other living child, Marcos, lives in this colonia too. He has talked about moving out to find work, but this dirt, these simple houses, own him as they do me. He will not leave. He loves this place too much. He loves trying to help teach the children English, trying to help them improve their lives in ways he has refused to change his. He talks with the mission people from the United States a lot; he is one of the few in our colonia that speaks English, although he says before too long the children will all be speaking it. I pray for him every day, for his happiness, for his soul.

I wave at the mission vans as they drive by. They have slowed down as they pass me, whether from the enormous ruts in the road or so as not to cover me with dust in their passing I cannot say. I prefer to think it is the latter reason, that they are not here just to hammer nails and feel good about themselves, that they truly care about the people in the colonia.

I think about how many of the twenty dollar bills line their wallets. It is ridiculous, that some can be so rich while others have nothing. I shake the evil thoughts from my head. These people have come a long way, to offer what help they can. I say a small prayer for forgiveness for so quickly forgetting my own blessings. Marcos always does what he can for me and Rosita sends me money almost every month. I am blessed, I truly am, to have children who look out for me.

I continue home. It is half a mile from the church to my little house. I smile when I think about how many times I have traversed the path between the two. Maybe some of those ruts in the road are from my bare feet, no? I laugh at the thought of my bare feet causing such issues for the vans and the trucks, that an old woman's twice daily journey could do such to the roads that man has built.

No one else passes me on my walk back to the house. Another hour before the children go running for morning school. It is a quiet morning, peaceful, still comfortable to walk in. That will change by noon, when the sun beats straight down, when the dust sits on your tongue so you keep your mouth closed. It will be warm today, with no breeze. Ah, ask God to keep the winds still so the dust does not blow through your house and then suffer the stillness without a cooling breeze. Such is life in the colonia, where whatever is happening, something else is desired. Whatever is built, something else falls to ruin.

I cross the threshold to my house, a thin rusted piece of barb wire strung across a few boards stuck in the ground serving as my fence. The yard is bare dirt, the grass long trampled underfoot. I smile when I think of the years my family has spent in this house, when Jose first brought me here, to the town of new hope, new progress, new beginnings. It has ended up like all the other little colonias, full of second and third generations of the same people, the same lives, the same dreams that are covered with rusted tin roofs. Yet it is my home, and I cannot bear to think of moving away from it. That rock, beside the door – it was where I sat, nursing Rosita, watching the sunset and waiting for Jose to come home. That hole in the side wall – that was where Marcos and Rosita would try to spy on our love making. This concrete block serving as the step into the house, I can still see Jose laying it down before me, promising that there would be poured concrete steps leading into a mansion for us someday. Someday. Someday.

Ah, an old woman dreams of the past because she can no longer see the future. I know when that changed, I know when my wrinkles formed, when my memories were brighter than my future. I remember all too well the day when Jose left me forever. It was days of fever and sweating before he became too ill to sit up. Then I knew that I had to find the doctor. But we had no money, we could not buy the medicine that may have fought off the infection that took his life. Even when I offered all we had, offered our very house, the doctor scoffed at us, said it was worthless. By the time I found another one, persuaded him to come out of the goodness of his heart, it was too late. The doctor took one look at Jose, shook his head softly, and walked away.

Screams from the road break my reverie. I rush as fast as I can to see what has happened. It is Carlotta's youngest, Felipe. He has fallen and a sharp board has pierced his side. His sister is wailing beside him. Carlotta comes running, one of the other children must have gone for her. She soon joins her daughter in tears and wails.

I take her by the shoulders, shake her hard until she calms down enough to listen to me. "Go, go fetch Marcos from the schoolyard. He will be able to borrow a car and take Felipe into town."

I take off my sweater and wrap it around Felipe's midsection, trying to stem the flow of blood. I send his sister into my house to fetch a pitcher of water, more to stop her cries by keeping her busy than for anything else.

She comes back and I tell her to go on to school, that her mother will want to know where she is, that she is safe. I send the other children that had remained watching along with her, instructing them to make sure she gets to school.

I dip my scarf into the water and wash Felipe's face. "It will be okay, Felipe." He moans with the pain and I look down the road, praying that Marcos will arrive in time.

The boy is still breathing, though he is suffering greatly, when Marcos comes bouncing down the road in a pickup truck. It is Ferdinand's, the man who goes into town and brings back water to sell us. I am surprised that Ferdinand would loan it to Marcus, I did not know he had a heart, as much blood as he charges for the water he sells.

Marcos does not waste any time, merely picks up Felipe and lays him in the passenger seat of the truck. I give him the twenty dollar bill that Rosita had sent me. "Take care of him, Marcos."

"I will, Momma," he promises.

I walk back to the church. A Rosary for Felipe, for Marcos and Rosita, I promise. And another one for you, God. Please, please let the boy live. Be it Your will, oh God, let the boy live.

M arcos

Morning school session will begin shortly. A few of the children are here already, playing around in the schoolyard. Someday there will be more than old tires and a patched up soccer ball for them to play with. Someday this will be a real school, with proper classrooms and computers on the inside, with swing sets and seesaws on the outside.

Maria runs up to me, chasing the soccer ball. She bids me hello in Spanish, I answer in English. I do not want to replace our language, but the reality is evident. Those who learn English will have a chance to better themselves. Those who do not are most likely going to remain in this colonia until they die.

I am not saying that one way is better than the other. My mother, she loves this place, would not leave it for anything. I love the people more than the place. The place I love is the one with the new school building, with roads that do not swallow a car, with running water that does not sicken the babies, with houses that do not let in the wind or rain. That is the place I love, that is the place I dream of. That is why I remain here, teaching children who would rather be playing a language they would rather not speak.

But I want them to have a choice. I want them to be able to go elsewhere and succeed in a variety of things, or to remain here and help create the colonia that I dream of. If they choose to remain but do not improve themselves, do not find a way to improve the basic quality of life in this place, then all my efforts are wasted. In that case, I would have been better off following Rosita to the United States, getting paid more in an hour than I make in most weeks.

I miss Rosita, I miss my little sister. Ah, and her children, I have not seen them since they were infants. I want her to visit but I know the money is not there. What little she can spare comes to Momma, I have seen her letters, have eaten meals provided by the money that comes with almost every letter. Rosita has not forgotten us. I only wish we could all be together. The only place that could come true would be in the colonia of my dreams, where Momma would be happy to live, I would be joyful to be a part in creating, and Rosita could have enough food for Margarita and Julio.

A woman comes running down the dirt road, howling and yelling out my name. It is Carlotta. She has two children that attend the morning session. She rushes up to me, and I must shake her before she calms down enough for me to understand her.

"It is Felipe," she cries. "He has hurt himself, badly. Your mother said you would help, could take him into the town to the doctor."

I look around. All my friends with vehicles, the ones that live in the houses near the school, are away, either working or looking for work. The only vehicle I see is the faded red pickup truck that belongs to Ferdinand, the water seller. He must not have left for the day yet to get a load of water bottles. I run over to the truck. I see the keys are in it. I do not see Ferdinand anywhere, there is no time to search for him. I jump into the truck and speed off down the rutted roads, bouncing so much as to hit my head on the roof of the truck.

I slam the brakes down hard and slide to a stop outside my mother's house. She is holding Felipe in her arms. The boy does not look well at all. There is blood soaking through the sweater that Momma has wrapped around him. I pick him up and place him on the passenger seat. I turn and Momma is standing there. She gives me a twenty dollar bill and tells me to take care of the boy.

"I will, Momma," I promise. I run to the driver side and get in, put the truck in gear and speed off down the road.

I look over at Felipe. The blood is oozing through the sweater that is wrapped around him. I hit a pothole and the truck bounces high. I turn away from the boy to concentrate on the road. It will do him more harm if I get a flat tire, there is nothing I can do for him other than to get him safely to the doctor in town as fast as I can.

I am halfway down the block when a man runs into the middle of the road. I place one arm across Felipe to hold him still while I press down hard on the brake. It is Ferdinand, he is yelling and waving his arms at me. He comes around to the driver side and yanks the door open.

"What are you doing, Marcos, taking my truck?"

I lean over, let him see Felipe in the passenger seat. "I am sorry, Ferdinand, I had no choice. I did not see you around, the boy is hurt, I must get him to the doctor while there is still time to save him."

"I have water to deliver, I have people counting on me, too, Marcos. I cannot let one boy stop my business."

He pulls me out of the truck. I clutch at his arm. "Please, Ferdinand. He will die."

He spits on the dusty road, scowls at me. "I suppose, if you will pay for a fill up for the tank, I could take you and the boy."

I will not have any money for the doctor if I pay him for gas, but that will be a worry for when we get there. I nod, get into the truck on the passenger side. I take off my shirt and try to rebind the wound as Ferdinand puts the truck in gear and drives us into town.

Once we get out of our colonia the roads improve. I do not think that Felipe is conscious anymore, the loss of blood too much for him to remain awake, so the bouncing has not caused him any additional pain. It is only about ten minutes to the town at the speed Ferdinand drives. He swerves around a couple slower cars and trucks, honking the horn and barely avoiding oncoming traffic. At first I think it is his concern for Felipe's health that causes him to drive like a madman, but one look at his grinning face as he pulls back into his own lane with little room to spare, and I know he would drive like this whether or not the boy was bleeding in his truck. I know he is enjoying this hectic drive, that he is glad to have found money for gas, and could care less about Felipe.

It doesn't matter. I don't care about his motives, his empathy, lacking or otherwise. As long as Felipe gets to the doctor in time, then I will say a prayer of thanks for Ferdinand's manic driving. The boy remains motionless in my arms, the blood now seeping through the shirt I tied around him.

"Hurry," I tell Ferdinand. He grins, dares to laugh as he presses the accelerator pedal to the floor. Minutes later we get to the outskirts of Progresso. Ferdinand quickly decelerates.

"The police, they know my truck, Marcos," he explains. "We cannot let them stop us."

Perhaps I was wrong, perhaps he does care about the boy.

"I think they will take my truck if they catch me speeding again."

Perhaps not. His truck! Not a thought of Felipe. "Just get to the doctor, Ferdinand." I bite my tongue, before I say more. This is not the time to get into an argument with him.

Two blocks later he pulls into the parking spot outside the pharmacy, where the only doctor in Progresso has a room in back. I tell Ferdinand to open my door so I can slide out with Felipe in my arms. He is asking me for the gas money, I tell him to hold the pharmacy door open first, that I will pay him once the boy gets to the doctor.

One look at us and the attendant runs into the back room calling for the doctor. I follow behind her. Gloria, that is her name. I have been here before, two months ago when Momma was sick. Gloria helped me find the right medicine for her. I did not have enough money to have Momma see the doctor, so Gloria helped me without charging for anything beyond the medicine.

We are at the door to the back room, Felipe in my arms, Ferdinand trailing closely. It opens and the doctor is there. He quickly inspects Felipe while I hold him, then turns and walks back into the room, motioning for me to follow him.

I lay Felipe gently down on the table inside the bright white room. There are more electrical lights in this one room than our whole colonia, I think, where a handful of families have a thin electrical wire running into their one room house, connected to an outlet where perhaps a single light is plugged in, or for the rich among us a stove.

The doctor looks at Felipe, checks his wound briefly, then looks over to Gloria, where she is standing just beside the door. "Gloria, please take the men out into the waiting room, and handle the papers."

"Will Felipe be all right, doctor?" I ask.

He shakes his head. "I cannot answer that yet. He has clearly lost a lot of blood. I will do what I can. Now please, I must have room to work. Go, wait outside. Gloria will get you settled in. It will be some time before I know whether or not the boy will make it."

My brief rise in hope at having made it to the doctor's goes out in a rush at his words. If he will make it? After bringing him here, Felipe still might not make it? I stand motionless, until a gentle tugging on my arm stirs me. I blink, see the hand on my arm, follow its slender arm up to Gloria. I let her lead me out to the waiting area inside the main pharmacy room, Ferdinand once again following close behind.

I sit down on a hard wooden chair. Gloria goes behind the counter and comes out with a pad of paper. "Is this your son?"

"No, just a boy from the colonia. He fell while playing... I guess you see what happened."

She nods. "Will his family be able to pay?" She bites her lip. "I'm sorry, I have to ask."

I look into her dark eyes. She cares for this boy, cares about the people who come in for help. I knew she had given me a discount when I came here for Momma. Now I see that if it was her choice, it would have been free. "Gloria, they have no money." I reach into my pocket, pull out the twenty dollar bill that Momma had given me. There is a red smudge on the corner, I guess some of the blood had soaked through my pants when I was carrying Felipe.

"Here," I say, extending my hand. "It is all I have."

"What?" Ferdinand shouts. "You must pay me for gas, Marcos. You promised!"

Gloria turns to him. "Sir, you were the one who brought these two in?"

I see her charm working on him. She tilts her head, the loveliest face in the town, smiles at Ferdinand. "You helped save the boy?"

Ferdinand is trapped, looking at the money and then up at her sweet lips and compassionate expression. He stammers, then swells his chest and declares, "Yes, it was I. I knew the boy was dying, that only a masterful driver such as myself could have brought him here in time."

Gloria clasps his hands in hers. "Thank you, sir. It was the kindest, most charitable thing you could have done. To have given the boy a ride to try to save his life. You are most generous."

The air leaves his chest as he realizes there is no way he can ask for the money now. He smiles, tries to make the best of it. "Ah, yes, Gloria, that is what I have done. From the goodness of my heart. Ferdinand is a most generous man, everyone knows that."

"I can see that." She writes down a brief note on the pad of paper, tears off the top sheet and hands it to Ferdinand. "Now, could you please take this to the Estencio Pharmacy – it is just a block down the street. We will need more medicine for the boy, I do not want us to run out. Just hand it to the attendant, she will prepare the medicine while you wait."

He looks at the paper. She puts her hands on top of his again. "Please hurry, Ferdinand."

"Of course, Gloria." He holds the paper firmly in one hand and marches out the door.

Gloria turns to me, looks down at the twenty dollar bill which I have been holding out during her whole exchange with Ferdinand. She smiles. "Now then, I believe that should cover the boy's medicine."

G loria

I have been working for Hector for almost a year now. Once he realized I was a good worker, and interested in medicine and not his advances, everything has been fine. I think the previous attendant had those interests reversed, and he may have gotten less work done but been at the office a lot more then — that is until his wife found out why he was working so late. She was around a lot the first month after Hector hired me, but I think she can see I have no interest in him as a lover. Not that there is anything wrong with Hector as a man, other than his wandering eye, but he is at least ten years older than I am, and not the sort of man I wish for a husband, especially since he already has a wife.

I spend most of my time reading his books. I am trying to save up enough to go to a university, but it will take years to earn the money for tuition. And it is hard to save, when so many people come in here needing medicine. They can usually only offer a tenth of what I am supposed to charge. Most of the time I have to turn them away, but when the need is great, when a child's life is at stake, how can I refuse them?

Hector gets mad at me when I am unable to collect the full fee. Sometimes he will offer his services at no cost, but he insists that the medicine be paid for. I understand. He has a family to take care of, a business to run. If he did not charge, then soon there would be nothing here at all.

It has been a typical day, with a few people coming in for medicine, regular patients that have used up their supply and finally got enough money to buy more. That changes when the door opens and two men walk in, the second one a young man, shirtless, carrying a bleeding boy.

I run back to tell Hector. He is about to go out when they arrive at the door to the back room, where we have the long table and what medical instruments Hector has been able to buy so far. Hector takes a look at the boy and then sends me to take the men back out to the pharmacy. As I lead the younger man, I realize it is Marcos. He has been here before. He is handsome. He lives out in one of the colonias. Although I met him but briefly a couple months ago, I have thought about him many times since then.

It is clear the other man is quite unlike Marcos. I learn his name, Ferdinand. He is more interested in getting paid than what happens to the boy. It is easy enough to stroke his ego, convince him he is a generous benefactor, a kind man with a big heart. I make up a list of medicines and send him to Estencio's. Marcos is hurting, concerned about the boy, and I find myself wanting to comfort him. I would rather do that without Ferdinand in the room.

After Ferdinand struts out like he is on a mission to save the world. I pull my chair over close to Marcos. I take the money he has offered.

"That will cover his medicine," I tell him.

He looks up at me, his face streaked with dust and tears. He has blood over much of his chest and his arms. "Will Felipe live?"

I reach out, place my hand on his arm. "I'm sorry, Marcos. I don't know. Hector will do everything he can. He's a good doctor. If there's anything that can save the boy, he will do it."

He nods. "Thank you."

"Tell me about the boy."

Some of the pain leaves his face. "Felipe, he is a good boy. One of my brightest students. He already knows more English than half the boys that are older than he is."

"You teach at the school?"

"Yes, I try. It is hard, there are never enough supplies. Many children sit on the floor. We make do with what we have, it is what we have always done at the colonia."

I knew that Marcos was different, that he was someone special. I feel my heart quicken as I sense his passion, his love for the children, for helping them learn things. "What makes you stay there? Why not teach in town, where we have books, paper, pencils?"

He shrugs. "There is nothing wrong with Progresso. But it is not my colonia. It is not my home. Besides," he says, smiling, his eyes not blinking once as they look into mine, "there are plenty of people who wish to work in town. But in the colonias – who wants to be out there, except those of us who live there? Those children, they need a chance, an opportunity to better themselves. If I can do that, then I do not care how many books we have in the school, or whether we have electricity or even chairs to sit on."

"You want to educate them, so they can have a better life – so they can find jobs in the big cities?"

For a moment, I see the hardness that is also within this man. He tenses, and I am a bit frightened at exposing something fierce where I had only seen tenderness. Then he relaxes and again I feel warmth coming from him, feel a stirring in my heart.

"No, only if that is what they want. I do not want to make them leave their homes. I want to let them be aware of what is out there, though, and to give them the knowledge, the wisdom, to decide if it is something they want. To let them survive out there if they choose to pursue it. But also to improve our colonia, to allow them to remain where they have grown up and hopefully help create a better place, a safer place. Not another Progresso. Just a better colonia."

I blink the tears from my eyes. I brush my nose against my sleeve. This man, this man could be the one, the one that I would want to share with. To be with. To marry. It is crazy, how little I know of him, or he of me, and yet as clearly as I would not be mistress to Hector, I would be anything to Marcos.

I stand up, turn around, before he sees me crying.

"What is wrong, Gloria?"

Too late, he must have seen. "Nothing," I say. "I just want to get something to clean the blood off of you. It isn't sanitary."

I go behind the counter, get some towels and some antiseptic wash. This costs more than he is paid in a day, I think. I don't care. I will not use that much. I can cover for it, if Hector even notices.

I dampen a towel and instruct him to hold out his arms. I gently wipe the dirt and blood from him. I hesitate for a moment when I finish with his arms. I look into his eyes, he again does not blink. I pour the wash on another towel and wipe it across his chest, staring into his eyes, wanting to embrace him, wanting him to hold me tight. Our breathing fills the room as I hold the towel against his chest.

I am not sure what would have happened. For a moment, we had forgotten everything else in the world, it seemed. But then the back door opens and Hector comes walking down the hallway. I quickly finish wiping the last bit of blood from Marcos' chest then step away from him. I can feel his eyes on me as I walk back behind the counter and dropp the towels into the basket to be washed later.

"How is Felipe?" Marcos asks, jumping to his feet.

"He is stabilized, for now," Hector says. "I have sutured the wound. He is still in bad shape, though. He should stay here tonight. If he makes it through tomorrow morning, he should survive. There's nothing else we can do but wait."

Hector turns to me. "Gloria, I know it is short notice, but can you stay and watch him over the lunch hour?"

I nod. "Of course."

"I will stay, too."

Hector looks like he is going to tell Marcos he cannot stay. I realize I want him here with me, I want to talk with him, to share this watch with him. This is something that could change my life – change both our lives – I realize. "That will be fine," I say, before Hector can tell Marcos otherwise.

Hector looks at Marcos, notices his cleansed chest and arms. He seems unsure. I stare hard at him, not giving any ground to his questioning gaze. "It will be easier to have someone else here, in case I need any help."

"If that is what you wish. But if anything happens, well, there really won't be much to do." He gives Marcos another look, then shrugs. "But as you want it. I am going to head home, then, for lunch, unless there are more boys falling on things? No? Okay then, I will see you later this afternoon."

Marcos approaches Hector, grabs his hand and shakes it firmly. "Thank you, Doctor. Thank you for saving Felipe."

Hector shakes his head. "We'll see if he is saved in the morning. You watch over my store, now. Keep anything from happening to it – or to Gloria. Understand?"

I flush at his inference, at his suddenly being the protective guardian over me. I have no need to worry over my embarrassment, however, as it is clear that Marcos is still shaken up over Felipe, and does not quite catch what Hector has said.

"I will do so, Doctor."

Hector nods. "Very good, then." He flips the sign on the door to closed. "Lock the door if you go in the back room," he tells me, as he leaves. I go ahead and lock it, knowing Marcos will want to check on Felipe soon.

I go behind the counter and find a white shirt that Hector has left there. I hand it to Marcos. "Here, put this on. We can't have you sitting here all day without a shirt."

I turn, suddenly shy. I could look at him bare-chested, but the act of slipping the shirt on, of buttoning it up, is more intimate, with us alone here. I turn around and he is done. He runs his fingers through his hair. "Can I see Felipe?"

"Of course, let's go back there now."

Before we get to the back room there is a banging on the front door. "Go on," I tell Marcos, "check on Felipe. I will take care of the door."

I head back to the front door. It is Ferdinand. He holds up a brown bag with one hand, waves through the glass with the other. I unlock the door and he walks in.

"See, I have brought back the medicine," he tells me.

"Very good. That will help so much, Ferdinand. Thank you." I try to be charming, try to flatter him, but my heart is in the back room now and I think he recognizes my insincerity.

"Where is Marcos?" he asks.

"He is watching Felipe."

Ferdinand frowns. "I have to pick up the water bottles. He must come now, so he can buy my gas. I am almost empty."

"But I thought you brought them here because—"

There is no softness in this man. My minor flirtations from before forgotten, he is again focused on his money. "I did what he made me do, he was stealing my truck. He is lucky I do not report him. I will go get him." He pushes past me and starts to go down the hallway.

"No, stop!"

He turns around.

"Marcos wants to stay and watch Felipe." I go behind the counter, open the register and take out the blood-spotted twenty dollar bill. Ferdinand comes back to me when I show him the money.

"What is this?"

"Just take it," I tell him. "Go fill up your truck, get your water bottles, just leave, okay?"

He smiles as he grabs the money from my hand. "You are a strange one, Gloria. But I have what I came for. Enjoy your schoolteacher."

I watch him go out the door. I rush over to it and lock it behind him. I walk to the back room. I slowly open the door. Marcos is kneeling beside the table, head bowed, murmuring prayers. I quietly sit in a corner chair and watch him. My schoolteacher. Maybe. Maybe so.

F erdinand

Man, what a waste of a day this has been. I should have been back at the colonia selling bottles of water by now, instead I am walking two blocks on the dirty street with a bag of medicine for the boy. The attendant at Estencio's looked at me strangely when I handed the scrawled list to her. She acted as if it was nothing special, nothing that could save a boy's life. Well, that does not matter. The other one, Gloria, she will reward me for this errand. I could tell by the way she looked at me, that she wanted a strong man to help her. Someone to press her close against his chest, to crush her underneath him after dancing and drinking in the cantina. She was a sweet looking one, with a fine body. It would be good to be with her, he was certain of that.

I already have her convinced I am a generous man, by letting her have the money from Marcos. She doesn't have to know that I will get that money back from him later. Marcos needs water at the school. He would pay me, or he would no longer get water. That would be easy enough to do. But for now, Gloria could think I was driving people around out of charity. Charity – hah! Why should I want to help others who were too stupid, too lazy, to make something of themselves? I worked hard to buy my truck, to build my water business up. Was it my fault if people like Marcos did not do the same? Or if silly women like Gloria thought that the weak ones deserved my assistance? No, I would have my fun with Gloria, and then get my money later. That is how it should be; hard workers should get the benefit of their efforts, should reap their rewards.

I get back to the pharmacy and the sign reads closed. I turn the handle but the door is locked. I pound on the door. I smile, hold up the medicine and wave at Gloria when I see her dashing down the hallway to open the door and let me in. Ah, she is eager to see me, that is good.

But then it changes. Her words ring hollow. I see she does not care for Ferdinand, no, her eyes are on another man. She actually cares for Marcos, it is clear to me. She has used me, sent me on a children's errand so she could spend time with him. I refuse to be made a fool. I will take the money from his flesh.

I start down the hallway to have it out with Marcos when she calls me back. I come back when I see the money she holds out to me. I remember how late it is, that the morning has passed. Better to take the money and go on with my business. I can always deal with Marcos later. I grab the twenty dollar bill and bid her good day.

I start the truck up and check out the fuel gauge. A quarter of a tank. That will take care of my rounds today, but since I am in town now it would be best to fill up the tank.

I head over to the water company first. The gas station is on the edge of town and I will stop there on my way out. I pull into the water company and park the truck. I go inside, sign for my usual number of bottles. This is what it means to be a businessman. To be able to go into a store, sign your name and be entrusted with the purchase. To have the respect from other people, for them to know you will make good with them. That is something a schoolteacher cannot do. They would laugh in Marcos' face if he tried to buy something on credit with his name.

I load the bottles into the truck. I count twice, making sure I have the proper number, not one bottle less or one more than I have signed for. A mistake in the count, and I am losing money or losing my account with them. The numbers match and I drive off to the gas station.

Pedro is sitting in a chair under the awning when I pull up to the pump. He gets up slowly, walks over, limping with each step due to his bad leg. He was hit by a car many years ago, and the leg did not heal properly. It doesn't matter much, I suppose, he has nowhere to go but from the chair to the pump and back. He is not a businessman, not like me — he is just a gas pump attendant, working for another man. I work for myself. I am no attendant.

"Good day, Ferdinand."

"Good day, Pedro."

"Five dollars worth?" Pedro asks.

That is my usual amount, the amount it takes me to operate the truck for a couple days. But today I have the twenty dollar bill, and it is always good to spend it on the business when you have the money, before some woman or bartender talks you out of it. "No, Pedro, fill it up all the way today."

Pedro smiles. "Very good, Ferdinand."

I walk over to the front of the garage. There are plastic crates with bottles of Coca-Cola in them, eight rows of eight bottles in each crate, with a dozen or more crates there. I decide that the businessman has earned at least a bottle of cola today. Better that than going to the cantina, where one bottle of beer would lead to another. I reach down and pick up a bottle. I glance around until I see the opener hanging on a string nailed to the side of the garage. I open the bottle, take a long drink, and return to the truck.

"Eighteen dollars, Ferdinand." Pedro notices the bottle in my hand. "And fifty cents for the Coca-Cola."

I hand him the twenty dollar bill. He limps back into the garage, comes out with my change. I take another drink from the bottle. It is sweet, not as sweet as those lips would have been, but I am a businessman, and this is a safer investment anyway.

P edro

It feels good, sitting underneath the awning on a fine day such as this. The breeze is gentle, the warm sun kept away by the shade of the awning. I amuse myself watching the cars and trucks drive by on the road. Occasionally one pulls into the gas station, and I have to get up and pump their gas. Most of them I know, there are few strangers with any reason to drive through Progresso.

A battered pickup truck pulls in and I recognize Ferdinand. The bed of the truck is loaded with water bottles, as usual. I get up slowly from the chair and walk out to him. I grimace as I walk. My leg is acting up again. Years ago a driver hit me when I was crossing the street. I could smell the liquor on his breath but he knew the policeman and nothing happened to him. Me, I still limp, and on some days, like today, the leg acts up and hurts when I walk.

I exchange greetings with Ferdinand. I am surprised when he asks for a complete fill up for the truck. Normally he does not have enough money to do more than get him through until his next collection day. I smile, glad of his fortune, glad that money is not a problem for this man that has been using my gas station ever since he started his water business.

I remove the gas cap and start the pump. Ferdinand walks over and gets a bottle of Coca-Cola. I watch his face as he takes a long drink from the bottle. That is a man who knows what he wants, and goes out and gets it. A satisfied man. A man with a strong body, two legs that he can stand firmly on. I feel a twinge in my leg as if it wants to tell me it is not its fault, it was not the one drinking tequila at the cantina and driving down the road afterwards.

I shut off the pump and replace the gas cap on the truck. I pat the leg. I know, that is just how life works. Some men are meant to be businessman, some are meant to sit under an awning and fill up trucks with gasoline.

"Eighteen dollars," I tell Ferdinand, "and fifty cents for the cola."

He gives me a twenty-dollar bill with a red smudge on one corner. I take the money and go into the garage. I open the register, place the money underneath the main tray. I take a single dollar from the tray along with two quarters and bring them out to Ferdinand.

"Have a good day, Ferdinand," I tell him. He thanks me and drives off with his water bottles jostling in the bed of the pickup, off to make his fortune. I return to the chair under the awning and rub my leg.

The rest of the afternoon passes with the typical cars and trucks stopping in. I sell another thirty or forty gallons of gasoline by late afternoon. Not a bad day's business, even if I am only the one pumping the gas. Around three o'clock a pickup drives slowly in, pulling a van behind it.

I recognize the pickup owner, he is from one of the colonias outside town, although I am not sure of his name. I watch him as he unhooks the van from his truck. There is a white man with him that I have never seen. I notice the van has Texas plates on it. I realize this must be one of the vans that I saw drive through Progresso early this morning.

The pickup owner walks over to me, the white man coming over and standing by me. "Hello, I am Carlos. This is George. He is with a missionary group that is building houses in our colonia. His van would not start. Can you help him?"

George offers me his hand. I see the sawdust on his arms and shirt, the dirt covering his face. I can tell he has been working hard today. I cannot understand how someone can have so much that they can come to another country and do what these people do. But that is their choice, I guess. What interests me is the van. I usually only get to work on trucks and cars.

I shake the offered hand. "Hello, George. I am Pedro."

He surprises me by answering in Spanish. A little difficult to understand with his accent and dialect, but he speaks it well enough that I can make out what he says.

"Hello, Pedro. Thank you for helping me."

I shrug. "We will see how much help I am after I look at the van."

I open the hood and inspect the engine. I have him turn the key, nothing happens. I poke around. I am pretty certain it is the alternator. I check a couple more things before going back to George.

"I need a new part. I will have to send for it, I do not have it here. It will cost one hundred and eighty dollars."

George sighs. He looks at Carlos. Carlos shrugs. "If he says he needs it, he needs it. Pedro would not lie to you."

I can tell that George was not questioning my trustworthiness – the look on his face is one of weariness, not of concern. George finally nods his head. "Do what you have to do; I have to get the van running again."

He turns to Carlos. "Can you give me a ride back so I can tell the others we will have to go back in two trips tonight?"

I realize he is going to leave the van here and come back for it after it is fixed. "Excuse me, George." He turns back to me. "I am sorry, but I must pay for the part when I order it. I need one hundred and eighty dollars to place the order or they will not send it to me."

This time I can see some concern in the man's face. But he sighs again, reaches into his back pocket and pulls out his wallet. He takes two hundred dollar bills and gives them to me.

"Thank you, George. I will be right back."

I go into the garage and retrieve the twenty dollar bill that Ferdinand had given me. I give the bill to George. "I should get the part in two days. It will take me half a day to put it in and make sure everything is running right. You can come back then."

George shakes my hand again. "Thanks, Pedro."

I nod. I turn away but then George comes back to me. He takes off the simple wooden cross that is hanging on a string around his neck. "Here, Pedro. Please take this, let it remind you that you are helping us out with God's work."

I hold the cross in my hand as George smiles at me again, claps his hand on my shoulder, then gets into Carlos' truck. I finger the worn wood as I watch them drive away.

G eorge

Things have been going pretty good. We are on the third day of our mission trip. We finished the first two houses this morning. After a quick lunch break we started framing the other two houses. Everything has been on schedule this time, we have been blessed with decent weather and so far an accident-free experience. No one has done more than bruise a thumb with their hammer or picked up a few splinters. God has been watching out for us.

This is my third mission trip. I swear, I get more out of it than the families we help out. We give them a better home, more room for their family, but the good feeling, the blessings in our lives, last beyond the seven days we spend here. I know it is not that much, what we do here, but every house we build gives another family more pride in themselves, a happier and safer environment to raise their children in. And oh, what children. The smiles on their faces, the beautiful, angelic creatures, they make your heart melt.

I realized we took both water jugs with us in our van after we packed up from lunch. We bring our own food and water each day. I know some of the workers have eaten the food brought to us by some of the families we help in thanks for our efforts, but my own stomach is not that strong, and I do not want to get sick from eating or drinking the local food and water.

The other work site is only a few streets away. I let Michael, our team leader, know that I am going to drop off a water jug to the other team. He asks me to bring back another can of nails.

I get into the van and turn the key. Nothing happens. I make sure it is in gear, try it again. Nothing. I catch myself from swearing. This is just one of those things, I think. The devil testing us, trying to turn away the goodness of our trip.

"Michael!"

He turns off the saw and walks over to me. "What is it, George?"

"The van won't start."

The rest of the crew walk over. There are seven of us on this site, six on the other team. None of us are mechanics. We raise the hood and pretend we know what we are doing for a minute before we close it, acknowledging it is out of our hands.

The mother of the house that we are building this ten-by-twenty attachment onto comes out to see what is happening. As I am the only Spanish speaker in the group, Michael has me talk with her.

"Our van is not working. Is there a mechanic or garage in the area, someone who can help us fix it?"

She frowns. "The only one is in Progresso. There is no one here in the colonia."

"Do they have a tow truck?"

She shakes her head. "No, but my brother Carlos, he has a truck. I will send Maria to bring him here. He can pull your van into Progresso."

"Thank you so much."

She calls her daughter from the house. Maria is the cutest little girl, probably only six or seven years old. She should be in school, but not all of the families send their children to classes. Sometimes it is due to money, sometimes it is just because they don't want to have anything to do with new things, I guess. I listen to the mother tell Maria to go fetch her uncle. I watch as she runs off, bare feet hardened and having no issues with the rough road surface.

I tell Michael that we are going to get a pull into Progresso. I will make the trip – the others will be fine here, and I can speak with the mechanic. Not perfectly, but enough to communicate.

Carlos drives up in his truck, Maria smiling as she is riding with him. He lifts her down from the passenger seat and you can tell she is feeling important, having successfully brought her uncle to us.

I thank her and she smiles and then runs back into the old portion of the house to hide with her mother. I explain the situation to Carlos.

"No problem, Mister George." He takes a rusted chain and hooks up the van to the back of his truck. I get in the passenger side and with a lurch that I am surprised does not pull the van apart we head into town.

When we get to the garage, Carlos introduces me to the mechanic. At least I think he is a mechanic. The man is older, and walks with a decided limp. But Pedro's eyes light up when he opens the hood to the van, and my doubts go away as I see him work around the engine. Either he knows cars, or he is a very fine actor. It is almost like he is caressing each part as he works his hands over them.

He has me try to start the van, and I am almost expecting it to roar to life after Pedro has touched the engine with such loving hands. But nothing happens. He tries another couple things, has me turn the key again, but it still refuses to do as much as click.

Pedro tells me I need a new alternator. I shake my head at the unexpected expense. Almost two hundred dollars. That's ten percent of another home for a family. That's two hundred dollars that won't go into a new tin roof, or plywood walls, or a floor for a kitchen.

I tell him to go ahead, to order the part. He stops me. He needs the money up front. I wonder if this is a scam, then shake off the suspicion. Another test by the devil, trying to get me to doubt a good man. Of course he would need the money up front. These people don't have two hundred dollars sitting around. I open my wallet. This money was supposed to buy groceries for the whole group when we got back to Texas tonight. Guess I will have to put those on the charge card. I'll figure out how to pay for them when the bill comes.

I hand him the two hundred dollars. He comes back with a twenty dollar bill and gives it to me. He tells me it will be a couple days before the van is fixed. That means shuffling our schedule. We will have to shuttle back to Texas tonight in the other van, then rent another one for a day or two until mine is repaired. We don't have time in our work schedule to spend an extra two hours making double trips twice a day to get everyone here and then back to the church where we are staying. Tonight will be a long one, but once we get another van rented we will be back on schedule.

Something happens every trip, there is always something trying to keep us from doing God's work. But God is all-powerful, and He watches over us. This could have happened at another site where we could not get a tow into town, or we could have found a mechanic who could not be trusted. Things happen for a reason, I remember. God's great plan is beyond our comprehension.

I stop before getting into Carlos' truck and go back to Pedro. I pull off the wooden cross that I have been wearing since Father Donovan placed it around my neck last Saturday morning, when he commissioned our mission team at morning mass, just before we left for Mexico. I hand it to Pedro, then get back into the truck. There, that is what I needed to do. I feel my van is in God's hands now, and despite the inconvenience I think it will all work out.

Carlos drives me back to our work site. The team has been busy in my absence. All the walls are framed now, with the window and door openings cut out.

Michael greets me. "You seemed to have left something behind."

I smile. "Yeah, the van needs a new alternator. The mechanic in Progresso is ordering it. It will take a couple days."

"I meant your cross."

"Oh." I smile, thinking of it resting in Pedro's calloused hands. "I gave it to Pedro, the mechanic. It seemed like the thing to do."

"We have more back at the church. If you felt you were supposed to give it to him, then I am sure it was for the best."

"Looks like you guys have done well. I should take off more often."

Michael nods. "Yeah, once we had you out of our way we could get things done!"

We both laugh. Michael turns to Carlos. "Thanks for taking our van in, that really helped us."

"No problem," Carlos says. "You are building a house for my sister, I could not refuse to give you a lift. Please, let me know if you need anything else."

"Thanks."

Carlos gets in his truck and drives off. I turn to Michael. "We'll have to shuttle in the other van to get back tonight. I figured I would rent another van for tomorrow."

Michael shakes his head. "We've got a couple hours left for today. I think we can get a couple of the walls up. Why don't you walk over to the other site — get Frank to drive you back across the border to get another van. Both teams will have a chance to get things finished for today while you guys are doing that. We'll be ready to head back over when you come back with the vans."

"That makes more sense." I walk over to the other site. It is always hard to walk through the colonia. You see so much more detail when walking than when riding in the van. The trash piled in the ditch on one side of the street, the standing pools of stagnant water, the broken rocks serving as lawns. It breaks my heart to see the state of some of the houses they live in. Little more than dilapidated boards with rusted tin roofs, not enough to keep out the rain or the wind.

I arrive at the other site and call Frank over. I inform him of what has happened. He tells the rest of the team we will be back in a couple hours and we head out in his van.

We get through the customs check without difficulty. We arrive at the rental place and I am able to get a full size van without difficulty. We quickly head back toward Mexico. Before we get to the border, Frank pulls into a gas station and I follow, parking beside him. He needs to use the restroom, preferring a questionable gas station restroom to the outhouse at the work site. I walk around the convenience store inside the gas station while I wait for Frank. I decide to bring the teams a little treat, since we are done for the day, and pick up a case of beer. Sometimes we all deserve a drink.

I dig in my pockets and fish out a twenty dollar bill for the clerk. I pass it over to him. Frank comes out and we get back in the vans. The beer is in a brown bag on the bottom of the van. I suddenly wonder if I am supposed to cross the border with alcohol. I decide it is best to declare it if asked, but the Mexican customs official just waves me through after a brief glance at my face, and I don't have to worry about it. That proves it, we are meant to have the beer.

K evin

This job is the best in the world. I get to sit here and watch TV for most of the day. Sometimes hot chicks come in, too. That's always cool. Almost everyone uses the Pay At The Pump now, so I don't even have to get up and pump gas, except for when they pull into the handicap spot and ask for service. Even then, that only takes a couple minutes. Yep, I lucked out when I got this job.

My friends always want me to sell them stuff at a discount – usually the five-fingered kind of discount. I tell them no way, I ain't going to get fired. This job is cake, not going to screw it up by letting my friends rob the place. I flip the channel. Jerry Springer's coming on, that show is a riot. I heard they paid people to be on it, but no way, those people are too freaking stupid to be actors.

A couple vans pull in. They park in the side lot. Bunch of free loaders, not even buying gas. One guy heads into the bathroom. Yep, just here to take a leak. The other guy wanders around. If he didn't look like Ward Cleaver I would be concerned. No, this guy isn't anyone to worry about.

He picks up a case of beer from the cooler. That surprises me, I would have guessed Diet Coke. Or lemonade. Anyway, he pulls out a twenty and hands it to me. I take a look at it, run our special marker across it. Standard procedure, nice guy or not the money has to be real for me to take it.

I give him his change, tell him to have a nice day and please come again. He thanks me like he thought I meant it. Geesh, can't he tell a canned employee response from something someone says for real? I smirk as his friend comes out of the restroom. The guy's wearing a cheap looking wooden cross, acting as if the world was all full of roses and sunshine. What a clown.

I turn back to Jerry after they leave. Someone's best friend is sleeping with her boy friend. Standard stuff. I open a bag of chips while I wait for the inevitable cat fight.

Two minutes of traded insults before the first swing. Then it is pulling hair and slapping. One of the girls grabs the shirt of the other one, and it rips off. Of course they blur out all the good parts. That's okay, I can always grab one of the magazines off the rack behind me to see that. I like watching them swing away at each other, and the bouncers pretending to hold them apart. If someone gets in a good blow they drag them away before any real damage is done. But five minutes later one of them will call the other a skank and it will start all over. It's good stuff.

A cute looking woman, probably about twenty-two or three, comes in. She's wearing short shorts and a tiny top. Got to love the weather in Texas, letting them walk around like that. I used to live in Chicago. Came down here for Spring Break last March and haven't left since. Beats the heck out of business classes.

I straighten up in my chair and turn down the volume on the set. She walks around, acting a little nervous. I can sense trouble. After the first two weeks at this job you start catching on to who the trouble customers are, by now it's second nature. But girls like this, they're the kind of trouble I like.

She finally grabs a few things from the shelves, random items. She approaches the register. She's short, about five feet even, but oh what a package. She sets down a bag of Fritos, a package of beef jerky and a National Enquirer on the counter. "Pack of Marlboros," she tells me.

She is looking past me at the cigarette display. I reach back and put the pack down on top of the paper. "Anything else?"

She doesn't look me in the eye. She keeps her head down, giving me an unobstructed line of site to her chest without worrying about her catching me looking. I like this girl. "No," she says. "That's it."

I ring it up. "Thirteen fifty-six."

She reaches into those tight shorts, digs a hand between the tightly pressed layers of denim and pulls out a hundred dollar bill. She puts it down on the counter. She fidgets as I take the bill off the counter.

I open the register, glance down at the bill marker. I look up and meet her eyes for the first time. She bites her lip, rocks back and forth. Oh, what a hot little woman this is, and yet she isn't like most women coming in here, thinking they are oh so much above me. She is scared of me, I realize. Frightened, nervous, unsure of herself. Not exactly how most women react to my presence.

I look at the marker again and it hits me. I know if I take that marker out, run it across the hundred dollar bill, it will not color up properly. She is passing a fake, and I know she is aware of the counterfeit nature of the bill.

"What's your name?"

"What?"

She is surprised, she was waiting for me to test the bill, wondering what would happen, and my question caught her by surprise.

"Your name. What's your name?"

"Jessica."

Her eyes are wide, I can sense her fear, smell her sweat as she waits to see what is going to happen. I smile at her. "I'm Kevin."

She doesn't say anything. She is confused now, not sure whether to run out of the store, to wait for me to test the bill, to confront me the way she would normally confront a gas station convenience store clerk asking her for her name.

I keep the hundred dollar bill in my left hand, reach out my right hand, which she takes by reflex. "Nice to meet you, Jessica."

She still waits. This is delicious, holding her in a trance like this, letting a hot girl like that wait while I control her fate. I sense a rush unlike anything I have ever felt before. But I know I cannot hold onto it, hold onto her – I have no delusions over the extent of my power in this situation.

I place the hundred dollar bill underneath the tray of the register. I count out her change, four twenties, a five, a single and forty-four cents. "Now that we've met I don't have to go through that silly testing. I only have to do that for strangers."

Her eyes open wider, her mouth hangs open a bit as she realizes what I've done, what I've said. She knows I know about the money, and she knows she's going to get away with it. She tenses a bit, as if waiting for the punch line, waiting for some kind of demand from me in return.

I smile. "Have a good day, Jessica."

She lets out a deep sigh, shaking as she smiles, thanks me, and walks rapidly out of the store. Watching her walk away was a sight to behold, let me tell you – it beat the ugly girl on Jerry Springer all to heck and back. I decide slipping the marker in my pocket would be the wise, so no one can blame me when they deposit the bill. Can't test a bill without that, I'll tell them.

Jessica

It's not going to work. This is crazy, I'm going to get arrested. But what else can I do? I've got to get some money, and this stupid bill that Jerry paid me with last week is the only cash I have. I could kill that s.o.b, passing me a fake bill. I almost died from embarrassment when the grocery store cashier told me it was counterfeit. Lucky I knew her, or they could have called the police then, or at least taken the bill away. I've got to find someone to cash it.

I think about the bank. No, that's stupid, even if they handle tons of money every day there is no way I could slip it in. Grocery store is already out, none of the bars I go to would take a hundred without testing it. Someplace smaller, that deals with cash but maybe doesn't test it. That's my only chance.

I walk into the gas station. There's a young man behind the register, looks like a greaser, dirty t-shirt and long hair. I walk around the store, trying to get up my nerve to go up to the register. I finally take a deep breath, grab some crap off of the closest shelf and go up to the register.

I don't want to look at him. I stare behind him. He's waiting for me to say something, I realize. I blink, try to focus on the display I was looking at. "Pack of Marlboros," I tell him, hoping my voice will not break. I don't even smoke, but I had to tell him something.

He reaches behind him and puts the cigarettes on top of the paper I grabbed. He asks if there is anything more and I tell him no. I pull out the hundred dollar bill from my short's pocket, feeling him watch me the whole time. I place it on the counter.

He picks up the bill, holds it in his hands like he can tell from the weight that it is not a real hundred dollar bill. Oh God, I am going to get caught, I am going to end up in jail. I am an idiot for even trying this.

He opens up the cash register drawer. I can see a marker in the drawer, the same kind of marker the cashier in the grocery store used. Dead meat. I bite my lip, wondering what story to make up, how I can try to talk my way out of this, wondering if I just turn around and run whether he will chase me down.

He asks me a question. I blink, ask him what he said. He wants to know my name. "Jessica," I tell him. What does it matter if he knows my name? Once he marks the bill it is all over anyway.

He introduces himself, then sticks out his hand. I reach for it automatically. He continues his small talk, and I am starting to wonder what is going on. Is he trying to hit on me? Does he think I am acting like this because I am attracted to him?

After a long time he releases my hand. He puts the bill in the register and counts out my change. He tells me we're friends now, that he can trust me. Oh my God, he knows the bill is fake and he is going to take it anyway!

I don't feel any safer. In fact, now I am even more worried. He wants something, they always do. He is going to ask me for my number, or to go for a drink, or maybe even to step into the back room right now. And if I say no the marker will come out, the bill will show as fake, and he will call the police.

But then he doesn't do any of that. He smiles at me, tells me to have a nice day. I cannot believe it. No strings attached, he is letting me go with my eighty-six dollars and change. I let out a sigh of relief but then I just want to get out as quick as I can and I do my best to not actually run out of the place. I get outside and go to the side of the gas station and throw up.

I wish I had something to wash my mouth out, but I'm sure not going back in there. I walk away, wanting to run, but afraid to draw any attention to myself. I make it to my bus stop and sit down on the bench. Despite the warm sun I feel cold, feel exposed to the world in my tube top and shorts. I still taste the vomit in my mouth. I keep telling myself that it's okay, it's over – that I have some money now, and I don't have to worry about anything. I suddenly jerk at the thought that the gas station probably had a video camera. They're going to run the tape, find out who gave them the hundred dollar bill. They'll post my picture on the news and the police will come and find me. I try to calm down, to remember the greaser's smile when he told me to have a nice day. No one will report it. No one will come after me. He won't turn me in.

The bus pulls up and I get on. The driver eyes my legs as I go up the steps but I ignore him. I take an empty seat and stare out the window at the streets as the bus circles the city. Once I get home I can brush my teeth, take a long hot shower to wash the stink of everything off of me. Once I am clean I can go on with things.

I pull the cord when we near my stop and the driver brings the bus to the curb. I get out, knowing he is watching me walk down the steps. I consider turning around and flipping him off but don't have it in me today. I walk the two blocks to my building and go upstairs to clean up.

After the shower I feel human again. I change into a pair of jeans and a t-shirt. Nothing tight, just regular clothes. I want to feel normal again, not like some little floozy strutting her stuff and turning guys on. Not another dancer in a smoky bar with a gravelly-voiced announcer telling the men to give it up for Candy. God, if I ever put on another cheerleader outfit...

But eighty-six dollars isn't going to last me long. I have to decide tonight. Do I go back to the club, face Jerry and tell him I'm sorry, tell him I was wrong to call him a pig, let him grab me without fighting back when I walk by him at the club? Is that what I want now? Is that who I am − Candy, pole dancer, smiling at the leering faces, ignoring the grabby hands as I coax dollar bills from their wallets? God help me, that is who I see in the mirror.

I look at the money on the vanity. I think about the greaser − Kevin, that was his name. He seemed happy in his minimum wage job. Happy enough not to give me a rough time, when he had me in a tight spot. If he was anything like Jerry he would have used that situation, would have forced himself upon me in some fashion. But he wasn't like Jerry; he was just an average guy, someone normal, that you wouldn't look at twice. Someone like I wanted to be again.

I grab the money, go into the bedroom and pack a bag with anything that has any real value. A couple pairs of jeans, some shirts, pictures from back home. I write a note for my roommate telling her I would be back in a couple days. I need to see my family. I need to get things set right inside again. I tape the note to the refrigerator and head back to the bus stop.

I catch the bus and stay on until it got back downtown to the main depot. I walk to the greyhound terminal and find the bus schedule. It was going to take all my money to get to Nashville. Mom and Dad keep on saying I don't visit often enough. Might as well take them up on it.

I go up to the window and pay for the ticket, getting only a couple dollars back. I thank the woman behind the window and head out to the terminal to find a bench to lie down for a couple hours until the bus leaves.

I count the meager amount left – enough for a sandwich and a cup of coffee, maybe. Well, Dad and Mom would have to buy my ticket back. If they don't want to do that they'll have to put me up – I'll let them figure out which way they want it. Either way, I'm going home. I can hear the music coming from the living room radio already.

Sharon

"Seventy-eight dollars," I tell the young woman. She pushes the money through the hole in the bottom of my bullet-proof window. I pass the ticket to Nashville back to her. She is a cute one, looks like she comes from a place like Nashville. Bet the boys are wild about her. I remember how that was. Don't let my current looks and age fool you – forty years ago, I would have put her to shame. I would have, I tell you. I was a real looker.

Now, well, now my hair is grey and my skin is flabby and spotted and things are in a different place than they were in my younger days, if you know what I mean. It's been a long life, a good life, but now things are a little harder. Harder to walk, to get around, to make it from day to day. Back when the boys were falling over themselves helping me carry my bags or open the door for me, those were the days all right. I couldn't lift a finger, they were so eager to win me with their helpful ways. And well, to be honest, there were a few times when they were not disappointed.

But that was so long ago. Ever since Jack left with his secretary, I haven't even looked at a man. Who needs them, now, when all they want is someone younger and prettier and perkier? God knows that isn't me, not anymore. But in my younger days, oh boy, was it ever.

So without Jack and his money, I had to go out and find a job. Me, after being a housewife for twenty-five years. It was bad enough that Jack took off without even filing for divorce, without giving me a moment's notice, but when I found out the bank accounts were empty and the house was double mortgaged to the hilt, well it left me in ruins. A younger woman might have found another man to help her recover, but I knew there were no sugar daddies out there for a woman of my age and looks. I had nothing, I had no one, but myself. So I sucked it up and hit the pavement and after a couple weeks found this job at the bus station. Selling tickets isn't glamorous, but it keeps me off my aching feet and provides enough for food with a little bit left over to buy some new shoes or a nice shirt every once in a while.

Another person comes up to the window. He is in his mid-thirties, looks tired, as do most of the people who come to the bus station. Rested people have their own cars or ride in cabs or planes. Poor people, hard working people, tired people – those are the ones who come to my window.

"Hello," I tell him. "How can I help you?"

"I need four tickets to Nashville. Two adults, two children."

I enter the ticket information into my screen and tell him the total. He slides a VISA card under the window. I run the card through my reader. A decline message comes up. "I'm sorry, that card is not being accepted."

He looks flustered. He asks me to try it again. I do, and the same transaction denied message appears. I shake my head. "Do you have another card?"

"No. No, I don't. Um… hold those tickets, please, I'll be right back."

I watch him walk over to a bench where a woman and two boys are sitting. He talks to the woman. They seem to argue a bit but then she reaches into her purse and hands him some money. He comes back over to my window and passes the money to me.

I check the two hundred dollar bills with my marker. I never look at the customer when I do this, I think it is rude to check their money, but rules are rules and I have to do it. I smile when the proper coloration appears. I place the money in my cash drawer and count out his twenty-seven dollars in change.

"There you go, sir." I slide the change and the tickets under the glass. "Have a nice trip."

"Yeah, thanks," he says.

I watch him walk back over to his family. The woman says something to him. He reaches into his pocket and hands her the change. Good for her, I think. Keep track of your money, or you won't have any at all.

D^{on}

Today has been another rough one. Mary has been mad at me. I tell her it's not my fault the company cut my job. It's not like I was the only one let go, half my division got the pink slip. She says I should have known it was coming, that I should have planned better, should have saved more money, so we weren't forced to head back to Nashville and move in with her parents. I say it's just until I can find work again, but there's no arguing with the woman. She wants me to shoulder all the blame. Like it was my decision to move down here in the first place, or to have two kids, or spend the money on that Vegas vacation last year. She doesn't seem to remember who wanted to do all that, except when it is convenient for her.

I ask David and Kyle to behave while I head over to get the tickets. An older woman, reminds me of my Aunt Polly, is sitting behind the thick glass window. "Four tickets to Nashville, two adult, two children," I tell her. I slide my VISA card under the window. Her smile fades as she reads something on her computer screen. Oh crap, it must have hit the limit, when we paid for the boxes to get shipped to Mary's parents.

I ask her to run it again but I know it won't go through. She slides the card back to me. I tell her to hold on to the tickets and head back over to Mary and the kids.

"The card's maxed out."

"What? How could you let that happen?"

I want to shush her, to tell her to keep her voice down and not make a scene, but I know that would only make it worse. "I'm sorry, honey, I guess the shipping charges added up higher than I thought."

"So what do you want me to do about it?"

I wait. Nothing I say will help, I have to let her work it out. Asking would be the wrong move.

"You don't mean... oh, how could you expect me to spend my birthday money on this? Daddy sent that for me!"

"Mary, I'm sorry. I don't have anything else. The card was rejected, I'm tapped out." I lean over, keep my voice soft, pleading. "Oh honey, please. I'll pay you back as soon as I get work, I promise I will."

She sighs, opens her purse, pulls out two hundred dollar bills. "Here. But don't think I won't remember it."

I know you won't, I want to say but have the good sense to keep it in. "Thanks, honey."

I go back to the window and slide the bills under the window. The lady smiles at me, wishes me a happy trip as she gives me the tickets and the change. I put them in my pocket and go back to the bench.

Mary looks up at me. "It's okay, I got them."

She opens her purse, looks back up at me. I sigh, reach into my pocket and give her the change from the tickets. She will still expect a full two hundred dollars back, as soon as I get a check, I know that.

I sit down between David and Kyle. "Okay, boys, we have a little bit of a wait. How about we play a game?"

I hug them close, and we start to play guessing games. I catch Mary listening in on our game. I whisper to Kyle to ask Mommy to play, but when he does she shakes her head, says she wants to read her book instead. I notice she still smiles at Kyle and David's silly guesses, and even some of my own. The smile, that is how she caught me. If only she smiled more often. If only she was still the person I fell in love with. I know it's possible, that the caring, smiling, laughing person is still inside her. I only wish I knew how to bring it out for more than an instant, for more than just a simple reaction to our four year old son trying to say banana without giggling.

M^{ary}

I am trying to read my book. Kyle and David are fussy. "Hush, be still boys. Daddy will be back in a minute with the tickets." They settle down for about ten seconds before they start acting up again. "Boys!" I get another page done before Don comes back. He looks shriveled up, like he has no spine. I wish he would carry himself straighter, would act more like the man I met back in Nashville. The one who had no qualms whatsoever about coming down here for the job with a startup company, the one willing to take risks to make it big. Now, now he was like a shadow of the man I fell in love with.

It does not really surprise me that he has maxed out the card. He never could manage money. I try to keep things in control, to budget things so we can do the fun things that we deserve, have a nice car, a nice house, enjoyable vacations, but no matter what I do he seems to find a way to ruin the budget. It's all I can do to keep a little money aside so I do not have to do completely without the little luxuries that make life worth living. If a girl can't get a massage at a day spa once a month, well, that would just be wrong.

I realize he expects me to pay for the tickets. Actually, not expects so much as needs. I think about what I wanted to spend the money Daddy sent me on, but I guess I can get more from him when we get to Nashville. Daddy won't stand for his girl being kept like a pauper's wife. I hand Don the money and start reading again. Once again the boys disturb me, and I barely get another page read by the time Don comes back to our bench.

I look up at him. He is being his usual clueless self. Does he really think that I would believe the tickets cost exactly two hundred dollars. I open my purse up, let him figure it out. He gets a little red in the face and then gets the change from his wallet and gives it to me. I place the money in my purse and close it. It will be an hour or so before the bus leaves. I open the book back up and try to concentrate on the story.

Don starts playing his guessing games with the boys. The sound of the three male voices, Don's bass, the boy's high voices, tripping over animals and cartoon names is a pleasant enough background noise. I find myself thinking of better times, when we would sit on the porch swing, when Don would play those silly games with me, trying to win me over with his humor. I look up and see the man I fell in love with is still there, sitting between our children.

Kyle asks me if I want to play. "No, Mommy wants to read. You guys go ahead." I do not want to be an active part in this, I don't think it would be the same. I want to listen in, though, to soak those voices in as I pretend to read my book. I want to remember how it was, when Don courted me, when days were good, when we were in love.

The hour wait passes nicely, with Don keeping the boys from getting fidgety, with my memories of our happy times leaving me feeling warm. I surprise him, and me, when I reach for his hand as we walk to the bus. He grins and I smile back at him. The boys are happy, Don is happy, I am happy. Somehow, I don't care about the tickets anymore.

We get the boys settled into their seats. They fall asleep before too long. I tap Don on the arm. "Don, I'm sorry."

"For what, Mary?"

"For being a witch. For not offering my birthday money from the start. I knew we were short on money. I should have let you have it from the start."

For a moment I think he is going to cry, and I know my tears would come a moment later. Instead he leans over and kisses me. It is everything that his first kiss was, on my Daddy's porch swing back in Nashville. I surrender to it and when he releases me my tears are wet, not with his tears but with my own drops, mixed equally of joy and regrets.

"I love you, Mary," he says.

"I love you, Don."

"It's going to be better, back in Nashville. It will be like old times."

"I know, Don. Just like old times." I let out a little laugh. "I was never a Texan, anyway."

He smiles, squeezes my hand. We sit together like high school sweethearts all the way to Nashville. The boys sense our happiness, they are bouncing up and down when we finally get off the bus, eager to stretch their legs. I grab David's hand, Don takes Kyle's.

We walk together to the McDonald's across the street from the bus depot. I call Daddy from a payphone and tell him we are there. He says he'll pick us up in half an hour. Don and I decide to get the kids something to eat while we wait. "Whatever you want," I tell them. I pull out the twenty dollar bill from the change at the bus station. I press it into Don's hand. "Daddy's buying," I say. He smiles at me, then passes it to the teenager at the cash register after she rings up the kids' two Happy Meals and a couple drinks for Don and I.

D enise

I swear to God I am going to kill Dean. For the third time tonight he has forgotten to drop the French fries so I have eight people screaming at me for their orders. How much intelligence does it take to hit a stupid button so the fries go into the hot grease?

I tell you, I am glad I'm not night manager. It's bad enough running a register and trying to keep the orders in line. If I had to figure out how to get the rest of these morons trained I would quit. They can't even figure out the difference in the cup sizes. Every box is labeled, every storage unit is labeled, every dispenser is labeled. You would think these people don't read English. Maybe that's it, they should label everything in video game instructions. Tell them there are cheat codes hidden in the labels, then these freaks would have the whole place memorized.

Someone comes up and complains that their plain cheeseburger has cheese on it. I try to explain that it's not a cheeseburger if it doesn't have cheese, it's a hamburger, but they don't seem to understand. I give up, ask them if they want buns around their plain cheeseburger and they tell me not to get smart with them. I give them a plain hamburger in a cheeseburger wrapper, and throw in a coupon for a free small fry with their next purchase and they go away sort of happy. 'Sort of' is about as good as I shoot for here.

So the lady walks away with her hamburger-in-a-cheeseburger-wrapper and fry coupon and I check on the burgers sitting in the heating tray. I toss the ones that are over the time limit. I know I don't want to get something that has been sitting under a heat lamp for half an hour. Besides, we have little tabs with numbers on them that tell us when to toss them. I usually do it, because clearly no one else here can tell time, except when it is time to clock out.

A couple comes up with two kids. Typical evening crowd. They look a little happier than most, but for all I know they are in the middle of a divorce. They get two Happy Meals for the kids and two large drinks for them. I gather the food on a tray and slide it to them. I give him the total and she passes him a twenty which he then hands to me. I count out the change, place the receipt on the tray and they head over to a table.

Ten minutes later one of the boys is back. His toy from the Happy Meal is broken, the tiny car only has three wheels on it. I wonder how this toy even got into the program – I'm surprised some little kid hasn't figured out how to chew the wheels off if they can break like this. Looks like a lawsuit waiting to happen. I save the corporation from going into bankruptcy by selecting a different toy, less apt to be swallowed, from the box underneath the counter. The kid is all smiles and runs back to his table where he shows off the new plastic wonder to his brother. I can't help but smile at how happy it made him. He'll probably lose it before they get home.

Another family comes in. This one is bigger, but not in number. There are two adults, probably pushing three hundred pounds apiece, and two kids, who will no doubt be there in a couple years. I am not surprised when they order everything super sized, including the Diet Coke, of course. Yeah, that's a couple calories that will make all the difference, on top of your two Big Macs and bucket of fries.

The guy hands me a fifty dollar bill and I count out his change. I can smell him from across the counter, it is obvious it has been more than one day since he showered last. I give him the change and the three trays of food. I look at the clock. Another four hours. Going to be a long shift. Not that there are any short ones.

D ustin

Took the wife and kids to a bluegrass show tonight. Nobody special, just a couple local bands, but they were decent. Kids liked it, Susie seemed to have a good time, too. I enjoyed the fiddle player in the second band. He had a way of sawing at that thing and smiling and letting you know he would rather be doing that than anything else.

I wish I could play like that. Hah, imagine me, Dustin Larnber, up on a stage with a fiddle. It would look like a toy in these big mitts. People would laugh at the sight, a former Division I lineman up on a stage, dancing around with a fiddle. Former. Yeah, that pretty much sums it all up. Former lineman, starter for two years before the knee blew out. Former potential second or third round draft pick, from what the scouts told me. That's okay. Who knows where I would be, even if the knee had held in that game against Tennessee? I could have been hurt anytime, I could have fallen in the draft, I could have been cut my first year even had I made a team. Coulda, woulda, shoulda. Former – I say formerly I would have cared about that.

But now, now I got Susie and the kids, Darrin and Heather. I wouldn't trade them for the starting right tackle position in the Super Bowl. Sure, we eat at fast food joints instead of fancy steak restaurants, but I get paid enough to sell cars at Dwyer's Chevrolet. The locals remember back when I could play, it helps get a few customers in and after a couple years I think I've turned into a pretty good salesman to boot.

I put one hand on each of the kids, loving how they lean against me, with my hand resting on their shoulders. I need a third hand to bring Susie into the group. I smile at her as she looks over the menu. I know what she is going to order, but she still looks over the menu every time we come to a place. She is thinking about getting a salad, she is always worrying about her weight. I tell her I love her, all of her, and I don't want any skinny model that is going to break when I give her a hug. Still, she worries, but in the end she orders a Big Mac and super size fries, just like I knew she would. I order two of the sandwiches, the kids get burgers and fries also.

The teenage girl behind the register looks vacantly at us when I hand her the fifty for the food. I wonder where her spark is, where the shine in her eyes has gone. It's sad to see someone so young look so listless, look like she has been behind that register for thirty years. I smile at her and thank her, wish I could give her a tip to make her day go a little better, but that just isn't done at McDonald's. She'd probably think I was a dirty old man trying to start something with her. That's about as funny as me on stage with a fiddle.

Susie and I carry the trays back to a table. We get a booth. It's a little bit of a squeeze for me but I am not sure their chairs will hold me. I've broken a few of them in my time, it's not the most pleasant thing to do in a room full of strangers. Although in the better restaurants you end up with a free meal most of the times. I guess they don't want to upset a former lineman, bad knee or not.

We dispense the burgers and fries and everyone is digging into the food. "Hey, want to go for ice cream after this?"

The kids light up at the suggestion. Susie frowns, she's thinking about her weight, I see her looking at the loaded burger in her hand. She looks up at me.

"Susie, it's okay. It's just ice cream. You can get a yogurt if you want."

"Yeah, come on Mom, it's just ice cream," Darrin says.

"Yeah, Mom, you can get a yogurt if you want," Heather adds.

Susie and I crack up. It's something the kids have been doing lately, copying everything I say to Susie. It takes a minute or two before we stop laughing. Other customers keep giving us the evil eye, but hey, if a family can't have fun at McDonald's, well, what's the point of eating out as a family then?

Finally Susie takes a drink from her pop and nods. "Okay, we can go for ice cream. But I'm getting yogurt!"

That starts the kids laughing again. My Susie, God I love her. Now that we have ice cream to look forward to, we don't linger around the table as long as we normally would, sitting and talking. We finish eating and clean up the table, putting the garbage in the bins and placing the trays on top. We head out for the car and drive over to the Ice Cream Shoppe.

There's another teenager behind the counter at the shop. This one is everything the other teenage cashier wasn't. She's bright, bouncy, acting like she is enjoying every minute of life. That's how teenagers should be. Most of them don't have to worry about working forty hours, or where they will sleep at night, or where their next meal is coming from. They should be carefree and happy, that is part of being young, of being a teenager. Missy, that's what her name tag reads, just seems happy.

"Hello," she greets us when we come in. She is a little plump – not plump by my family's standards, but by the super anorexic model standard that is pushed on young women. She has dark brown hair with streaks of red in it and pretty brown eyes with all the sparkle missing from the McDonald's girl. This was a girl you wanted to have around you, she brightened the room with her smile and cheerfulness.

"Hi," I say.

The kids press their noses against the display glass that covers the tubs of ice cream. Susie looks at the menu, scanning the yogurt offerings, but I see her glancing down at the tubs behind the glass, too. I lean close behind her. "It's okay, Susie. Get what you want."

She looks over her shoulder at me and smiles. She surprises me, though, and stays with yogurt. I get a double scoop of mint chocolate chip, Darrin gets a scoop of chocolate with sprinkles on it, and Heather orders the daily special, some mix of chocolate, peanut butter and white chocolate chips.

Missy is actually humming while she scoops out the orders for us. She smiles and says "Here you go" as she passes each cone over the counter to the person who ordered it. After we all get our ice cream and yogurt, I pull out a twenty dollar bill and pay her. She gives me one more smile as she hands me my change, saying "Thanks for stopping in, please come again," and I believe she means every word.

M issy

This is my second week working at the Ice Cream Shoppe. It's a lot of fun. Everybody who comes in here is in a good mood, I mean they are getting ice cream after all and who doesn't love that!

I especially like handing the cones to the little kids. It makes me wish I had a little brother or sister but it's just me at home, well me and Dad. Mom took off a couple years ago but we don't talk about her anymore, that was her choice and it doesn't mean she didn't love me or even Dad but just something she felt she had to do. Dad and I get along just peachy without her, though sometimes I catch him staring off into space, looking all sad. Those times I sneak up and give him a big old hug and then he smiles and everything is okay again.

It was hard, the first year after Mom left us. It's been a lot better lately, I even talked Dad into asking the woman who plays the piano at church out to a movie last week. I don't think they are going to fall in love or get married but it was sweet to see him standing in front of the mirror and checking his hair. I even ironed a shirt for him to wear. When he got home – way too early, there's no way they went for a drink or even a slow drive after the movie, he was back before eleven o'clock, you won't catch me coming in that early after a date – we talked for a bit and he said she was nice but he didn't think they would go out again. But he didn't say he wouldn't ask someone else, he didn't say that at all, so I think before too long I'll be able to find the right woman for him. That piano player was a little too conservative anyway, he needs someone to perk him up a bit. Someone who doesn't mind that I put streaks of red in my hair or that my nose is pierced.

The owner of the Ice Cream Shoppe, Morgan, is real nice about that stuff. He says as long as nothing is hanging loose where it can get into the ice cream he doesn't care what I wear or how I look. I still know he prefers it a little more conservative so I do my best to look like a nice, clean cut teenager, because he was nice enough to hire me without any experience, and I want to do my best for him. Morgan is a sweet old man, probably twenty years older than Dad. He and his wife, Trudy, come by almost every day and have their scoop of ice cream and to visit with whoever is working. That's what I want for my Dad, someone that he can spend time with and enjoy going out with, someone to care about him as he gets older. Because much as I love him, I don't plan on being his babysitter after high school. Nope, this girl has to get out there in the big old world and have some fun. I'm thinking Europe. I'm thinking that, not saying it out loud, because I'm not so sure Dad would be keen on his little girl backpacking around Europe on her own. We'll see how much I can save over the next two years. That will determine whether I need him to help out, or if I can swing it on my own. I heard it was cheap if you stay in the bed and breakfasts and get a Euro rail pass.

A couple comes in with their two kids. They look like they enjoy their ice cream quite a bit, if you know what I mean. But gosh they look like a happy family. I smile and tell them hello. The dad, a big old teddy bear, I bet, smiles back and tells me hello right back. The kids press against the glass, checking out all of our thirty-two tubs of hand-dipped ice cream. We do have a lot of flavors, and I like almost all of them – the ones with nuts in them I could do without, but everything else is yummy. I almost giggle when I see the kids sliding their faces across the outside of the glass, making sure they see each and every flavor before they make their choices. I just want to give them a scoop of everything and see them go crazy!

But I can't do that, it wouldn't be good for them to eat that much ice cream, so I wait for their orders. I do put a little bit extra in each cone, making sure they get a nice sized scoop of their flavor selection. They all smile and thank me and then the dad pays me for the ice cream – oh, and for the yogurt, I guess the mom is trying to eat healthier. Personally, I would rather skip part of supper and get the real stuff for dessert. I give him the change and tell him to make sure they come back. He smiles and nods his head and I bet I do see them again.

I put the money in the cash register. Morgan will be by in a bit, right at closing time. He always locks up the place and takes the day's receipts with him. I told him I could lock up for him if he wanted but he just grinned and gave me a look as if it would be the silliest thing in the world for him to have someone else lock up his ice cream store. I guess if you care about your place of business it isn't a job to do that, it's something you want to do.

I watch the kids eat their cones, licking their lips and their ice cream covered fingers when they are done. It is good to see kids enjoying their ice cream, it reminds me of when I was little and Dad would pick up a half gallon and he and Mom and I would sit on the back deck and eat just about the whole thing. I can't remember the last time we sat out back, the last time we shared ice cream together. That's kind of sad.

The family leaves and I look up at the clock. Twenty minutes until closing time. I sweep the floors and tidy things up. No one else comes in until right at nine o'clock Morgan comes through the door. I would normally call him Mr. Broomfield but the first time I did that he gave me a real stern look and waved his finger at me. He said, "Young lady my name is Morgan don't you go 'Mistering' me." His stern face gave way to a big grin and we both started giggling and right then and there I knew I was going to love working at the Ice Cream Shoppe.

"Hey, Missy, how's my favorite girl doing today?"

"I'm fine, Morgan, but don't let Trudy hear you calling me your favorite girl or you're going to be in a mess of trouble."

He laughs. "Aw, Trudy doesn't mind. She knows I'm a silly old man who likes talking to pretty girls."

"Well, this pretty girl has had a good day. Last customers were a nice family, the cutest kids you ever did see. I just wanted to squeeze them and hear them giggle."

"Don't be squeezing the customers, Missy, they might squeeze back."

It's always fun talking with Morgan, he is pretty sharp, he keeps up with the one liners as fast as I can dish them at him. We talk some more about the day's business and then he puts the money from the register in the zippered bag he takes to the bank each morning. I try to pay for a half gallon of chocolate fudge that I want to take home – no nuts, just good old chocolate and fudge ice cream – but he doesn't take my money, laughs and says he'll write it off as quality research. He locks the door behind us and walks me to my car, a used VW bug that Dad helped me paint half a dozen different colors. It's a fun car to drive. I can't wait to get home and pull Dad out onto the deck. We've got some ice cream to share.

M^{organ}

I kiss Trudy goodbye. It's time to head to the Ice Cream Shoppe and close up for the night. I always like visiting with the young people that I hire. I wouldn't hire anyone that I wouldn't want to talk to, or doesn't seem to like working at the shop. Life is too short to be doing something you don't enjoy. Besides, it's my shop, and I think happy workers make happy customers, and happy customers keep the business going. I have customers that have been coming to the shop for fifteen years, ever since Trudy and I opened the place. Must be doing something right, with customer loyalty like that.

The new girl, Missy, is a fine example of the type of kid I want working for me. She's been nothing short of super since the first day she worked. Got a real knack for scooping, and a wonderful personality. You get a young woman like that behind an ice cream counter and you are guaranteed success, as long as you have a good product to go with her smile. And that is something I have never skimped on – I use the best ingredients, as fresh as I can get them, and I sure don't worry about having exactly one scoop in a cone – I tell the kids to pile it high, to keep the customer thinking they are getting more than they paid for. I don't mind getting a scoop or two less per tub than the industry standard. Standards don't make people happy.

We only live two blocks from the shop. I quit driving last year, Trudy hasn't ever driven. We don't need a car, not with the bus system. Nowhere else we'd rather be than where we've been living for thirty plus years. It's a pleasant evening and I wave at the people I pass. Most of them wave back.

I get to the shop. It's empty except for Missy. I note with pride how she has already swept up, and wiped the glass clean. She's a good worker. If I had a granddaughter, she would be just like Missy, I like to think.

We trade jokes and finish putting things away for the night. She has a half gallon of ice cream and starts to ring it up. See, even though I like all my workers, most of them would have just assumed they could take it home for free. Sure, they can, but it is nice to see her expect to pay for it.

"Oh, that's not necessary, Missy," I tell her. "I'll write it off as quality control. You have to inspect the product every now and then."

"You sure, Morgan? I don't mind paying for it."

I shake my head. "You trying to mess up my taxes? You put that money away!"

She laughs and does as I tell her. I gather the extra cash from the register and put it into my bank deposit bag. We turn out the lights and I lock the door behind us. I walk her over to her crazily painted car. Kids, they love making their cars stand out. It suits her, though, with the bright reds and oranges and yellows and the happy faces painted on the sides of the little bug car.

She waves goodbye as she drives off. I take a last look at the Ice Cream Shoppe, then walk back home. I have a spring in my step from seeing Missy. Being around young folks helps you stay young, I think. It sure works for me.

I get home okay. Trudy is getting ready for bed. I place the deposit bag on the kitchen table. I will go to the bank in the morning. I could just take it once a week, but walking there each day gets me more exercise, and besides I like the tellers at the bank. Go to a place three or four times a week for fifteen years, it gets like another family. I would miss them if I stopped going as frequently.

So the night is uneventful, other than the typical three a.m. bathroom visit but I don't need to dwell on that. All part of growing old. It's like a cycle, you spend as much time in the bathroom when you are old as you did in your diapers when you were a baby. But like I said, who wants to worry about that, it's just part of life.

In the morning, Trudy fixes me toast and orange juice. We read the paper, trading sections as we go. She likes the front page and the life section best, I enjoy the business and sports sections the most. We have nowhere special to go so we take our time, pointing out articles to each other and reading out loud any quotes that we find particularly amusing or upsetting. Politicians and comics, those are the ones that tend to get read out loud.

After finishing breakfast and the paper, I kiss Trudy goodbye. I never leave her without kissing her, you never know the day or the hour, and I would feel awful if the last time we had been together we had not kissed.

I walk the ten blocks to the bank. I wait in the short line, no more than five minutes. "Good morning, Alyssa." Alyssa has been working as a teller for about six years. She is always nice to me, I make sure to give her a pint of apricot ice cream, her favorite, at Christmas.

"Good morning, Morgan. How are you and Trudy doing?"

"Just fine, honey." I know some people don't like to be called honey, but I am an old man and I use it to my advantage. If I can't flirt with pretty young women – and anyone under fifty is young to me – then the heck with it all. Besides, they let old people get away with just about anything, as long as it isn't really hurting anyone. They just shake it off as being old fashioned or not knowing any better.

I pass the zippered bag over to Alyssa. She counts out the twenties, tens and fives — I always leave the ones at the store, you never have enough singles. She fills out my deposit slip for me, enters the information into her computer and gives me the receipt. I place my hand on her arm. "Thanks, Alyssa. You have a good day."

She smiles at me. "You too, Morgan. We'll see you tomorrow."

I smile and wave goodbye to the other tellers and Thomas, the security guard, on my way out. I get out onto the sidewalk and the morning sunshine is just beautiful, another glorious day to be alive and in love. I decide to go home and take Trudy for a walk. She'll like that, she doesn't get out often enough. I wave at all the people I pass on the way home. Most of them wave back.

A lyssa

My feet are killing me. I knew I should have brought my tennis shoes with me today. Stan, the manager, doesn't like us to wear tennis shoes but it isn't against bank policy unless we are sitting out in the customer area so there's nothing he can do about it. Besides, I stand behind the teller window all day, I could be wearing shorts and flip flops and they would never know it.

But my other shoes are in my bag right beside the door, where I had left it thinking I would surely see it and take it with me. Since I didn't I am stuck with this pair of flats that are not broken in properly and too tight in the heel, and I finally decide to just slip them off and stand in my bare feet.

Boy does that feel better and I think I did it soon enough so the headache that was just starting to form might not turn into a full blown migraine. If it does, it will be one long day. Doesn't seem to matter how many ibuprofen I take, they don't touch it when I get a migraine. Doctor Bennett says it is all in my head, ha ha, but he doesn't have any clue how it feels when your whole head is pounding so much you just want to jump off the top of a building to make it stop.

Thankfully, as the morning progresses the sensation dims. Taking off the shoes, or just feeling more relaxed – whatever it was, I am thankful and almost in a good mood without that concern. I've managed to avoid Stan noticing my shoeless feet, hopefully I can get through the morning without him seeing them and then I can run home at lunch to get my tennis shoes.

I cash a check for a customer and then I look up and see Morgan walking to my window. He's a sweet old man, comes in almost every day, ever since I've been working here. He even gives us all ice cream for Christmas, knows every one of our favorite flavors, could tell you off the top of his head. He's a smart guy, I think he was a big shot at a company downtown before he retired. His wife is in a wheelchair, I heard he quit his old company so he could spend more time with her, take care of her himself. She doesn't get out much, but when he brings the ice cream she usually makes it for that trip. She's a nice old lady, looks like she would break if the wind blew too hard, though.

Morgan flirts with me as usual. If someone like Stan called me 'honey' he'd see the back of my hand faster than he could blink, but Morgan doesn't mean any harm. It's just his way, and he is so sweet and loving to his wife that it disarms anything he may say about my pretty eyes or about heading down to Acapulco with him for the weekend. He jokes with all of us, all the women anyway, about heading off on an exotic getaway. He always says we have to get back in time to tuck his wife in!

I count out his deposit and fill out the slip for him. I know he can do it himself, I think he purposely fails to fill it out so he can spend more time talking with us. I don't mind, he's nice and I would rather have ten of him than most of my customers. You never have to deal with complaints about the wait or service charges with Morgan.

He thanks me and waves goodbye. I place the money in my drawer, making sure each bill is facing the proper direction. There's a red smudge on one of the twenties. I look at it but it is nothing serious so I put it in the drawer with the others.

A couple hours later a young man comes in. He cashes a check for two thousand dollars, tells me he is going on a business trip. I give him fifteen hundred in hundred dollar bills, three hundred in fifties and the rest in twenties. I have to get the hundreds from Stan, who checks the signature on file for the account. I pull the fifties and twenties from my drawer.

I count out the money on the counter in front of the customer. He doesn't smile, doesn't flirt, just watches carefully as I place one bill on top of the other. He places them all in a bank envelope and leaves without as much as a thank you. He'll never own an ice cream shop or have someone he cares about like Morgan does, I think.

The day passes without anything going wrong. Stan doesn't notice my shoes, and I am able to get my tennis shoes at lunch, so no migraine forms. All in all, a pretty good day. At the end of the day we double count the drawers, making sure all the totals match. I hand over the money to the floor supervisor and he takes it all to the vault. I put on the flats to walk back out to my car and head home. I leave my bag with my shoes in the car this time. I won't want to forget them tomorrow.

D ennis

Two thousand dollars. That's what it is going to cost me to get Vincent off my back. You would think visiting your brother would be a happy thing, but with Vincent it's always one thing after another. Sure, he loaned me ten grand two years ago, and I had promised to pay him back, but didn't I send him five hundred dollars just last year? The man simply had no sense of brotherly love.

He's been bugging me about it a lot lately. I think Rebecca is the main reason. They've been getting serious, thinking about getting married. Rebecca wants a nice ring and a fancy wedding so I have to suffer and cough up some cash for Vincent.

I'm driving up to Chicago this afternoon, so I stop in and cash a check. I just got paid my bonus for the quarter so I guess the timing is good for Vincent, though it will pretty much drain my account. I go into the bank. The teller is one cold fish, not that she is much to look at anyway. I'm going to hit rush hour traffic, I can tell. It doesn't help that she is counting the money out like she's worried the bank alarm will go off if she goes too fast. I grab the money and stuff it in an envelope and place that in the inside pocket of my jacket.

I get into the car and head for the freeway. Going to be a long drive. I find a classical station on the radio, anything but this twangy music they force on you almost everywhere in town. Man, I need to get back to a real city. That's what this trip is all about, trying to get reconnected with my old boss in Chicago. I needed a place to crash, should have known that Vincent was going to hit me up for more than the hotel would have cost. I guess I was hoping he would have let it go, since he knows I'm trying to get a new job. It's Rebecca. If it wasn't for her he wouldn't be asking me to pay back a dime.

I cruise up through Indiana. Nothing but cornfields. Man, what a waste of four hours. I guess I won't hit rush hour because these yokels won't get over in the slow lane and I'm not making very good time cruising up interstate 65. Figures, won't get into Chicago until past seven o'clock, probably won't get to Vincent's until eight. Oh well, he'll probably have something in the refrigerator for me. That's one advantage to him dating Rebecca, he usually has more than pickles and beer in his refrigerator now. That's about it, though. I don't know what he sees in her, she's just another gold digger wanting to put her claws in him. Six months, that's what I give them, and then she takes half his money and gets alimony until she finds the next sucker. I tried to tell him that on the phone but he hung up on me. What are you going to do, try to do your brother a favor and look out for him and he bites your head off. If it wasn't for how she was changing him, turning him from being somebody that would bail a brother out when he was down on his luck, I'd say good riddance to them both. But he's my brother, I can't give up on him. No, you just don't do that to family.

Traffic is still a little backed up when I get to the outskirts of the Windy City. I roll the window down, breathe in the city smells, the exhaust fumes, the dirty air. This is a real city, no country town grown big around a bunch of twangy guitars and truck ballads. I'm going to find a way to get back here, even if Larry won't hire me back. Even if I have to move in with Vincent until I get settled. It'll be for his own good, really. I can set him straight about Rebecca. Yeah, I'll be doing him a favor.

Another hour or so and I pull into Vincent's driveway in a suburb west of Chicago. It's a small little ranch, one decent sized bedroom and two tiny ones. And no garage, I bet he is shoveling and scraping snow and ice off his car five days a week in the winter. He should have asked me before buying it, who buys a house without a garage in Chicago? Oh well, hopefully I will find my own place before the snow gets heavy.

I am glad to see only Vincent's car is in the driveway. Didn't want to deal with Rebecca, at least not until I get the guest bedroom locked up. I feel the envelope in my jacket pocket. Yeah, this shouldn't be too hard.

I knock on the door. Vincent opens it up. He looks at me, opens the door wide and steps aside, closing it behind me.

"What, no hug for your brother?"

"You got the money?"

I take out the envelope. "Here you go, Vincent. Two grand."

He opens the envelope, flips through the money. "You can count it if you want to."

Vincent smiles. "Nah, I trust you. What, my own brother, going to cheat me?" He comes to me and hugs me. "Good to see you, Dennis."

It is good to feel his arms around me. This is what I remember about my big brother, him protecting me, guarding me, keeping me out of trouble or getting me out of it when that didn't work. "It's good to see you, too, Vincent."

We break apart. We go into the kitchen, Vincent grabs two beers from the refrigerator and hands me one. "I got some leftover Chinese, if you're hungry."

I nod and he fixes me a plate. We sit down at the kitchen table and Vincent quietly drinks his beer while I eat. I finish quickly. He takes the plate and puts it in the sink, then sits back down.

"So, going to see Larry about your old job?"

I take a drink of beer. "Yeah, that's the plan. I miss this place. I can't stay down in Nashville, it's just not me."

"What if he doesn't have a position for you? You left him in a bit of a bind, the way you took off last year. Didn't even give the guy two week's notice."

"I'm hoping he forgot that part. Anyway, if he won't take me back I'll just keep looking."

"Oh." Vincent watches me as I take another drink. I don't say anything. After a minute he can't stand it. "So, where you staying, then? While you're doing all this job hunting?"

I smile, shrug. "I'll find someplace."

"Good."

"Unless…"

He doesn't bite. I have to continue on my own. "Unless I can use your spare room. I know I said it would be just for this weekend, but it would really help, Vincent. Just until I get a job, get my first check. Once I can get my own place I will be out of your hair."

He looks at me, shakes his head. "I don't know, Dennis. I'm getting pretty serious with Rebecca. I don't know if I need a third wheel around."

"Third wheel! Vincent, I'm your brother, not some bum off the street!"

He grins and I realize he was pulling my leg. He laughs, slaps his hand on the table. "Oh, boy, did I have you going. Of course you're going to stay here, Dennis. I wouldn't have you anywhere else. Besides, it will give you a chance to know Rebecca better."

I roll my eyes. "Yeah, that's what I need."

"Hey," Vincent says, reaching out and placing a hand on my arm. "I'm serious about that, Dennis. I love her. And I'm sure if you get to know her a little better you'll realize why I do. She's special, Dennis, and I'm lucky to have her. Just give her a chance."

"If you ask like that, how can I refuse?"

"Good. Now, let's talk about rent."

I laugh. "Not going to fall for it twice, brother."

He smiles. "It was worth a shot." He gets up from the table. "I've got to run down to the store – why don't you get settled in here. It won't take long."

"Sure thing."

I get my bags from my car. Vincent rolls down the window in his car as he is pulling out. "If Rebecca calls tell her I'll be right back, okay?"

I nod and wave as he drives off. I take my bags into the spare bedroom and start to unpack. The phone rings five minutes later. It's Rebecca. She seems nice enough on the phone, all eager and hoping we can go out for dinner while I am in town for the weekend. I think about how Vincent sounded when he talked about her, how much she meant to him. I change my tone and tell her it will be nice, that maybe we should meet for lunch tomorrow, get to know each other better. I tell her anyone that means so much to my brother means a lot to me, too. I can tell she is surprised, it is probably the first time I have ever spoken to her without underlying sarcasm. She agrees, says she would love to do that. I tell her Vincent will be back in a few minutes, and I'll let him know she called.

Maybe she is the one for Vincent. Maybe she isn't. But I guess this is one thing I won't screw up for him, not on purpose anyway. I finish unpacking, go back into the kitchen and grab another beer. I smile when I see the contents of the refrigerator. Not much more than pickles and beer after all.

V incent

It's good to see Dennis again. Sure, he's a screw-up and causes me a world of headaches every time he comes into town, but he's my little brother and I wouldn't have it any other way. He surprises me with the money. I didn't think I would see any of it. It was more of a threat, trying to get him to start saving some money, than an actual request for the money. It'll come in handy, but I will stash fifteen hundred of it away in my savings account, for the next time he hits me up for a loan.

I put the twenties in my wallet, the rest of the money back in the envelope. I place the envelope on top of my dresser. I'll take it to the bank tomorrow. I go back into the kitchen, get Dennis fed. It's nice to sit down and share a beer with him. I'm happy he's back in town where I can keep an eye on him. Hopefully he will stick with it this time. The boy's got restless feet, but the city always calls him back. He's never really happy away from Chicago.

I tell him to unload in the spare bedroom. It's why I have it, I always expect him to come back and crash in between whatever random idea has him traveling elsewhere. Maybe this time he will stay for good, find a job that keeps him satisfied, a good woman to keep him stable. Someone like Rebecca, if he's really lucky. Man, I sure hit the jackpot with her.

She likes the Bears, the Cubs, even the Jordan-less Bulls. What a woman. And so pretty, so caring, she makes me feel like I'm handsome, strong, rich — not that I'm ugly, weak or poor, but I reached for the stars when I went after Rebecca and boy did I catch one.

She's an executive vice president for a firm in the business district, don't even ask me what she really does every day. I met her at a Cub's game, we were talking about another All Star player they signed that immediately tanked when playing under the ivy in left field. By the third inning, she had asked me out to dinner and one date led to another and before we had time to catch our breaths we were in love.

I know she's going to call while I'm out. She wants to give me a cell phone so she can reach me when I'm not at home but I tell her ninety percent of the time if I'm not at home I'm with her and it would be a waste. I'm not much for gadgets. Other than widescreen television sets on Sunday afternoons for Bear's games, of course. But Lenny's bar down the street has that so why do I need one?

I head to the grocery store and fill up a basket with enough food to get Dennis and me through breakfast. Eggs, milk, butter, bacon, bread. That should do it. I pay for the items. Outside the store a man is hawking roses. I decide what the heck, Rebecca will probably come over later to say hello to Dennis. I hand the man a twenty in exchange for half a dozen semi-fresh flowers.

"Thank you sir, your lady, she will love these," the man says.

"Ah, as long as she loves me, she can throw the flowers away."

He laughs, thanks me again. I head out to the car and drive home.

P eter

I sell love. Oh, I'm not a male prostitute. No, what I offer to those I meet are flowers, the perfect symbol of love. The rose's bloom, the very fruit of nature, glorious, beautiful, representing the first passion, the first kiss, the first night a couple spends together. And then the flower wilts, the color fades, the petals fall one by one from the stem. But while it is fresh, while the bud is firm and the smell fragrant, how wonderful it is.

Every customer has their own story, just as every love has its own beginning, middle and end. Some are trying to start a new romance, when they buy my flowers. Those are the ones I like best. They tip better, and they take hold of the bouquet as if they are cradling their would-be lover's heart. Ah, fresh love, there is nothing like it in the world.

Some are just stoking long burning fires. A gentle love, a marriage of forty years, a friendship just as long. These are nice people but you know their night will end up with a kiss on the cheek and maybe even separate beds. No passion burns there anymore, they are beyond those years. Sweet, romantic, but not for me. No, I turn back to fresh love. Fiery, passionate, new.

Then the ones I like least, the ones I do not even want to sell my flowers to – the ones who have cheated, or failed their lover in one way or another. They think to bribe their way back into the hearts of their lovers, want to make their misdeeds go away as if love was something to be bartered with. My flowers are not meant for that, but what can one do? Even a flower seller must eat, and to be honest there are more flowers bought by the cheaters than the passionate ones and the romantics combined.

This man coming to me, with his sack of groceries, I can tell his is a new love. A romantic would not be coming to me second, after the groceries, and a cheater would be buying more than half a dozen. Besides, his face is flush as he buys them, not from embarrassment but from sheer joy at the thought of doing something for the woman — I presume woman, but these days even I cannot tell for certain the object of his desire — he loves.

We joke a bit and he is happy. He pays me twenty dollars, letting me keep the couple dollars change. I thank him and he goes off with his groceries and his bouquet. I smile at the thought of him presenting the flowers to his lover. Ah, fresh, new love, that is what keeps me going each day.

I am almost out of flowers. I decide to walk on down the block to the bus stop. I might as well head back home. I will sell a couple more, perhaps on my way.

No one is interested at the stop, but as I ride I sell three single roses to various passengers. The driver looks in the mirror a couple times but I never let him catch me. Silly city rules, trying to legislate the sale of love. It cannot be done, love is beyond the law. Still, I have a single rose left, waiting for a lover.

I get off at my stop. I walk along, looking for a customer for my final rose but no one is interested. I decide to drop in at the corner diner. I have not eaten since lunch and there is nothing but a pizza coupon in my kitchen. There are only a couple other people in the diner. I go up to the counter and sit down on a stool, placing my final rose on the stool next to mine.

A young woman comes up to me. She looks tired, but there's something about the way she manages to smile at me despite what must have been a long day behind the counter for her. She makes me believe she is happy to serve me, that this stool has been sitting here just for me.

"Hi, what can I get you?"

I smile at her and read her name tag. "Good evening, Claire. How are you tonight?"

For a second I am wondering if the question will annoy her, if she will frown and ask me again what I want or do I need a minute to look at the menu. But only for a moment, because I see my words actually cut through the grind of a waitress job in a tiny diner on the corner of a not so great location. She tilts her head, actually considers what I have asked. Finally, she smiles. "I'm doing okay, mister. How are you?"

I smile back, I can't help it, and I feel the stirrings of everything that surrounds me every time I sell a bunch of roses to a customer. "Now, now I think I am just fine and dandy."

I keep looking at her, not ogling but looking at her, and she blushes a little bit. "I'm sorry, I don't mean to stare, really I don't but you just seem…"

She smiles, her eyes bright, her head tilting again as she waits for my judgment. The words don't fit, I want to say fresh or nice or normal but nothing quite describes it properly. I let the silence linger too long, I guess, because her head tilts back straight and her smile turns down just a hair and she leans a little more away from me. She looks down at her order pad, clears her throat. "So, what do you want or do you need a minute?"

I order a grilled cheese sandwich and a side of fries. I watch as she takes the order back to the fry cook. What should I have said? What could I have said, that would have saved a moment like that, that might have changed things? What did I just miss?

I sit there, watching her while waiting for my food. She fills up my water glass without my asking, but she doesn't meet my eyes, she doesn't linger around my seat, or ask me to finish my sentence. Of course she doesn't. Once that moment faded away, I became just another customer, just another guy who tried to hit on her and she is probably regretting even giving me an opening.

I get the food and eat it slowly, wanting to stay here, wanting to somehow go back in time and recapture that moment, the moment when the bud just opened and the fragrance came bursting forth, when everything was fresh and new and all doors were open, when the possibilities were infinite. When love could have blossomed.

But there's no turning back the clock. A chance like that, it does not reoccur. You either seize it or it is gone, forever lost. You have to pray another moment comes, another chance with someone who you can connect with. You have to hope this was not the one you were meant to be with, your soul mate, your perfect match. But what if it was? What if you have just thrown it all away, and will regret it all your life?

I order pie and coffee, even though I am full. I cannot leave. I cannot walk away from this. I manage to eat half the pie before my stomach demands I stop. I drink three cups of coffee, delaying the inevitable, forestalling my exit.

She comes back, carrying the pot. "You need another fill up?"

I glance up. Claire. Her name is Claire. I realize I had to look at her name tag again, she had been transformed into a vision in my mind, beyond flesh and blood and human names. She seems tired, more so than when I came in. I wonder if she also has seen a chance lost, if her half frown is the result of her own disappointment in an uncompleted sentence.

I realize all may not be lost. Perhaps sometimes you can reach back in time, recapture that which was missed. Maybe destiny, true destiny, can handle a lapse in vocal ability by a foolish man too slow to find the proper words. I smile at her and it reaches through the last forty minutes of emptiness, for she smiles back. I place my hand over the cup. "No, no more coffee. I'm ready now."

C laire

It's been rough, working at the new diner. I lost my other job a couple weeks ago, when I was late for work for the third time in five days. I was lucky to find this one, even if it pays fifty cents less an hour. Now I'm stuck working week nights until I can work my way up the seniority chain again. That usually takes a couple months, it's not like this is a long term job for anyone here.

I wish the place were busier. It's bad enough getting the cut in my hourly rate, but when the tips are smaller and less frequent, well it doesn't quite add up to what I need to make the rent. I guess I need to find a roommate, but that's hard to do. Most of the people in the ads end up being psychos or perverts or drug users. I asked a couple of the other waitresses but so far no one is looking for a place to stay.

Well, I guess I'll make it. One way or another, everything always works out, that's what they say. I make another round with the coffee pot. I try to keep them filled up, they appreciate it since the refills are free. I don't think the owner likes us to pour without being asked, but I need the tips and the customers tip more if they don't have to ask. He can bump my hourly rate if he wants me to be stingy with the coffee.

A cute guy comes in and sits at the counter. I ask him what he wants and instead of rattling off his order he surprises me and asks me how I am doing. His eyes are blue and he looks like someone I would have found next to my locker in high school, a real nice guy. I actually think about it, think about losing my job but then finding one right away, about how life really does work out and decide that I am doing okay. He says he's doing fine and dandy, I smile at the words.

He keeps staring up at me and I realize it's been at least a minute since either of us said anything and I feel my cheeks turning red. He doesn't seem embarrassed at all, he seems intense, and happy. He keeps looking, then says, "I'm sorry, I don't mean to stare, really I don't but you just seem…"

I wait, wait for him to finish the line, it seems forever as I stand there with my order pad in one hand, looking down into his blue eyes. Another minute passes, he shifts his eyes away from mine and I wonder what the heck am I doing standing around wasting time. I ask him what he wants to eat and I write the order down and walk back and clip it on the wheel, spinning it around for Buck to take and cook.

I feel him watching me as I go around filling up coffee cups, taking orders and delivering them. Buck calls another order for me and I pick it up and it is his sandwich and fries. I place them in front of him and fill his water up again, refusing to look into those blue eyes. I won't be caught standing like a silly school girl again.

I clean up the dirty dishes from the counter and then he orders pie and coffee. He takes his sweet time, at least half an hour, working on the pie. I fill up his coffee cup three times while he keeps pushing the remaining portion of pie around on his plate.

Finally I go up to him, ready to fill his cup again. He covers his cup with his hand, looks up and I am caught by those eyes. Gosh, he's cute, take him home to Momma cute. He picks up the check from the counter and hands it to me along with a twenty dollar bill.

I take them up to the register, ring in the order and punch the check down on the spike with the rest of the day's orders. The money feels funny in my hand, and I take a closer look at it. A red spot in one corner, several markings on it, dirt smudges, a bit of grease. Just a regular twenty dollar bill, nothing special. I put it in the register and count out the change.

I go back to him and place the change beside his plate. He gathers it up. Not even a dollar tip, I think. Then he reaches out and presses all of it in my hand.

The moment he touches me thoughts of the tip are gone. The warmth emanates from his grip. I look into those blue eyes, find myself matching his smile. He reaches to the stool beside him and brings forth a single red rose. "My last one, Claire. I knew there was a reason no one bought it. It was meant for you."

I let the bills fall, the loose change clattering on the counter. I take the rose from him, lift the flower to my nose and breathe the fragrance in. I can't help it, I'm a sucker for romantic gestures, especially when they come from cute young guys.

He drinks eight more cups of coffee, staying until my shift ends. Then he walks me home, arm in arm. I carry the rose with my other hand. We get to my building. I want to invite him in, this blue-eyed stranger, but while I may be a bit loopy I am not completely insane. I do give him a quick goodnight kiss. I watch him walk away, he is humming some song I have never heard but I am sure it is a love song.

Like I said, life works out. Not how we planned, or how we think it ought to, but how it was meant to. I sure didn't think being late for work would have been the best thing to ever happen to me, not when it got me fired. Not when my new job paid less than the old one. But then Peter and his blue eyes showed up. Blue eyes, eleven cups of coffee and a single red rose. The rose may have wilted, but we haven't. Life works out. It's all a big circle sometimes –

sometimes maybe a circus – but grab it when it zooms by and ride that circle with all you have. Find your man, your coffee, your rose.

www.ingramcontent.com/pod-product-compliance
Lightning Source LLC
Chambersburg PA
CBHW051821170626
46807CB00003B/975